# The Alien Probe

# TOM SWIFT®
# THE ALIEN PROBE

VICTOR APPLETON

WANDERER BOOKS
Published by Simon & Schuster, New York

Published by WANDERER BOOKS
A Simon & Schuster Division of
Gulf & Western Corporation
Simon & Schuster Building
1230 Avenue of the Americas
New York, New York 10020
Manufactured in the United States of America
10 9 8 7 6 5 4 3 2 1



Library of Congress Cataloging in Publication Data
Appleton, Victor, pseud.
The alien probe.

(His Tom Swift; 3)
SUMMARY: An alien probe found wrecked on one of Jupiter's moons and containing insane "intelligence" is stolen from a laboratory before its secret of stardrive is obtained.
[1. Science fiction] I. Title.
PZ7.A652Al [Fic] 80-28768
ISBN 0-671-42538-2
ISBN 0-671-42578-1 (pbk.)

# CONTENTS

# Chapter One

Tom Swift stared, his mouth opened wide, and he slowly shook his head.

"No. That can't be!" he exclaimed. "That's impossible!"

He looked at his robot, Aristotle, aghast.

"I am sorry, Tom, but there is no longer any doubt. The alien probe is, to use a phrase applicable to humans, insane. I could not warn you any earlier."

Tom Swift stood up, stretched to his full six-foot height, and began to pace around his private laboratory. He and his friends, Ben Walking Eagle and Anita Thorwald, had returned only a few days before from a trip to the moons of Jupiter. On one of the moons, Io, they had discovered an alien probe.

Fortunately, Aristotle had been able to communicate with the probe, who said it was from a planet orbiting the star Alpha Centauri. It claimed to be a messenger sent to find intelligent life who could help its people—the Skree—defend themselves against a group it called the Chutans. In exchange for this help, the probe promised to reveal nothing less than the secret of interstellar travel—a stardrive!

The moon Io had been entering a period of intense volcanic activity and Tom and his friends had barely escaped with their lives, taking with them the alien probe's memory core.

Their trip back to Earth in the giant spaceship, the *Daniel Boone,* had proved somewhat frustrating for Tom. Though Aristotle spent all of his time with the probe, he seemed to get very little information from it.

The probe had been brought to Swift Enterprises' undersea Triton dome, off the coast of Florida, to keep it out of the public spotlight as much as possible. Top scientists from around the world would be arriving in a few days to study the information Aristotle had been able to gather.

Now Tom paced around his laboratory, incredulous at the latest information about the alien probe.

"Tell me again, Aristotle. Slowly. I want to make sure I'm not misunderstanding a word."

"I very seriously doubt that you misunderstood me. I repeat. Now that the alien probe's brain core is safely housed in a lead-shielded box in a blast-proof room, I can speak freely. It has been difficult for me to communicate with it because its logic circuits have been under great stress from its long captivity by the cooled lava of Io. The probe is, alas, quite insane."

Tom thought for a moment, then slowly shook his head. "How could that be possible?"

"Perhaps it was damaged during its landing on Io," the robot responded. "Or maybe the intense heat from the volcanic activity and the radiation from Jupiter itself warped some vital function. Or perhaps a combination of these factors plus others altered its circuits."

"Did the probe tell us the truth about life on other planets, or was it just some fantastic distortion? *Is* there an intelligent race out there in the stars? And if so, is it almost destroyed by a barbaric horde, the way the probe says? Can the probe deliver what it promised, a true stardrive?" Tom was clearly upset.

"I believe the probe is telling the truth about these matters," Aristotle slowly replied. "The malfunction from which it suffers does not seem to have affected its basic programing yet. Rather, it is confined to other areas. So far I have been unable to determine the exact extent of its damage."

Tom looked sternly at the mechanoid. "Why didn't you tell me this before?"

He went to the large laboratory table and sat down on one of the high stools. "If the probe is so dangerous, why did you allow us to bring it onto the *Daniel Boone*? That endangered the lives of hundreds of people."

Though he did not say so, Tom was beginning to think perhaps exposure to the alien probe's mind had affected Aristotle's circuits. Certainly allowing a highly dangerous, largely unknown *thing* to travel millions of miles with hundreds of unsuspecting people seemed to be a violation of Aristotle's programing.

"I am sorry," Aristotle responded. "I was not positive of the condition until we were almost back to Earth. I am a flawed mechanism. At first I thought my circuits just were not responding correctly to the probe. After several days of constant communication, it became obvious that the probe was severely disoriented. Besides, once we were aboard the *Daniel Boone,* the danger was significantly lessened," Aristotle added.

"How?" the young inventor asked.

"The probe's desire to fulfill its mission is very strong. If it had destroyed the *Daniel Boone* before its return to Earth, it could not complete its mission. That is why I urged the probe be placed in such protective housing."

"This is something we had been discussing with Ben and Anita," Tom said. "While I try and get them, you contact my father in his private lab."

Tom had met Benjamin Franklin Walking Eagle while working on his Prometheus drive. Ben, a full-blooded Cherokee Indian who was a genius with computers, had been Tom's copilot during a famous space race when their small racer, the *Davy Cricket,* had proven Tom's Prometheus drive would work.

Their closest competitor in the race had been Anita Thorwald, a saucy redhead. Her intense rivalry with the two boys had turned to admiration, though she remained frequently outspoken when she disagreed with them.

Tom began to punch out the sequence of numbers on his wrist communicator which would connect him with both Ben and Anita if they were within 100 miles of his lab.

Suddenly the harsh clang of the general security alarm sounded throughout the complex.

What's going on? Tom wondered. The general security alarm was only sounded for the most important emergencies, such as a seismic disturbance cracking the great undersea dome or a cargo sub in trouble outside in the clear Florida water.

"Tom, what's happening?" asked Ben's voice over the communicator.

At that moment Aristotle cut in. "Something seems to be wrong with the circuits into Mister Swift's lab. There is an intense static on all lines."

Tom turned to the robot who was busy at the small computer. "See if you can override the interference. I'll try to get General Information."

"Tom." Anita's voice was filled with urgency over the small wrist speaker Tom was wearing. "Sergeant Garrott in Security just contacted me. For some reason they can't get through to you.

You are to get over to your father's lab on the double. It's an emergency!"

"Thanks, Anita," Tom replied. "You and Ben had better meet me there. Aristotle has just given me some very disturbing news about the probe. I'm afraid we might have real trouble on our hands."

Tom and Aristotle ran out of the lab. They were on an upper level of the great geodesic dome in the residential decks. Mr. Swift's private lab was on the far side, lower down, nestled among the tanks and storage rooms of the giant undersea city.

The two slowed to hop through one of the many pressure hatches that cordoned the decks. The dome was, in many ways, built like a ship, with the ability to shut off decks and whole sections in case of flooding or other disasters.

The robot spoke as they moved rapidly down a corridor. "I am afraid I have more bad news," he said.

Tom dodged past a linen cart being wheeled in the opposite direction and headed down the emergency stairs, bursting out into a recreational area. Here, off-duty personnel and visiting sailors from the cargo subs mixed with tourists and other visitors buying souvenirs, trying their hand at games, getting their holograms taken, and wolfing down Neptuneburgers, fish sticks, and Seapop. "What now?" he asked.

"Someone deliberately jammed all incoming frequencies to your laboratory. That is why Security could not locate you. I was not sure before, but now that my circuits have fully analyzed all the available data, there can be no mistake about it."

The robot narrowly missed collision with a woman selling "authentic simulated gold pieces salvaged from sunken galleons." He followed Tom as the young inventor wove through the crowd like a field runner, swiveling his way deftly around startled tourists. Tom wondered why no one down here seemed at all disturbed about the alarm. Was it possible it had not sounded in this section?

The two rounded a booth selling necklaces of shark's teeth made in a Miami plastic factory and ran down a service corridor. Then they pushed through a plain door marked AUTHORIZED PERSONNEL ONLY and found a service elevator just arriving.

Breathing hard, Tom closed the door and thumbed the button for the lower section. He looked at Aristotle and asked, "Why would anyone only jam the incoming frequencies to my lab? They did nothing to interfere with the outgoing signals. I had no trouble reaching either Ben or Anita."

"Perhaps they were interrupted before completing the jamming process," the robot replied.

Tom bit his lip. Someone apparently had planned to prevent him from communicating with anyone outside his lab. Why? So he could not call for help during an attack? Perhaps his would-be attackers' plan had only been foiled by the general security alarm. The fact that the alarm went off might have saved Tom's life!

Aristotle would not have been able to defend him, because the mechanoid's programing strictly forbade him from hurting a human being.

What was behind the whole thing?

The elevator stopped and its two passengers dashed out and turned left, almost sprinting down a concrete corridor, through a hatch and into the hallway leading to Mr. Swift's private lab.

A burly security guard only glanced at the badge fastened to Tom's jumpsuit before waving them through.

Tom saw Ben and Anita a few yards in front. Before he could call to them, Anita went through the open door of his father's lab. Tom heard her gasp and call to Ben.

Seconds later Tom and Aristotle entered the lab. Mr. Swift was lying on the floor, blood splattered on his collar.

"Dad!" Tom yelled as he ran to his father's side. Kneeling, the young inventor reached out to touch his father, then stopped in shock. The older man was unconscious!

# Chapter Two

"Get a doctor!" Tom demanded.

Ben hurried to the computer on the other side of the room and punched in the emergency code.

"Mister Swift has been hurt," he said to the person who responded to the code. "We need a medical team at once in his private laboratory."

Tom did not dare to touch his unconscious father until qualified help had arrived. He knew that any move might aggravate internal injuries.

Anita and Ben looked around the lab which was now in shambles. A stack of library tapes had been toppled. Broken beakers and smashed electronic parts were scattered on the floor. A three-dimensional map of the Blake Plateau, the base of the Triton dome, was shattered.

The emergency medical crew burst into the lab and went to Mr. Swift.

"What happened?" one of them asked.

"We don't know," said Tom. "I was told to come here only seconds after hearing the general security alarm. When I arrived, I found my father like this." He moved away slightly to give the team room to examine Mr. Swift.

"General security alarm?" asked one of the team. "We didn't hear it."

Tom frowned, but before he could comment, Mr. Swift groaned and tried to move. "Tom?" he called weakly.

"Take it easy, Dad. Help is here," Tom reassured his father.

The older man's eyes fluttered open and searched for his son. "Tom . . . break in . . . probe—" he swallowed and breathed heavily.

"Please don't talk, sir," one of the medics said. "Time enough for that later. Save your strength."

Mr. Swift shook his head slightly. "Lieutenant Foster . . . stole . . . probe . . ." Then he lapsed into unconsciousness again.

The three friends stared at each other in shock!

"Ben," Tom said, "check with the storage area where the probe is housed. Maybe Dad's mistaken."

Ben went to the computer and punched the sequence.

"Tom," the leader of the medical team called out, "at first glance it doesn't appear to be too serious. We have to get your father to the sick bay. I want to take some X-rays, just to be certain. The concussion is probably slight, but we won't take any chances."

"The blood?" Tom asked anxiously.

"It's from his fall. The cut is not deep—we won't even have to use stitches."

Two medics gently placed Mr. Swift on a stretcher and began moving him out of the lab.

Tom was torn between finding out what had happened to the alien probe and staying with his father.

As if reading the young man's mind, the leader of the medical team kindly placed his hand on Tom's shoulder. "Call me in twenty minutes. There's nothing you can do for your father right now. We'll let you know as soon as there is any change."

"Thanks very much," Tom replied.

Anita and Ben came over to Tom after the medic had left. "The probe is not in its storage area," Anita said, her face tense. "The guard on duty says your father signed it out about fifteen minutes ago and said he was bringing it to his lab to run some tests."

"He must have surprised Foster, who jumped him and then took the probe," Ben added angrily.

"I thought he had been court-martialed," Anita said. "What's he doing here at Triton?"

Lieutenant Burt Foster had endangered the lives of Tom, Anita, and Ben through careless piloting on their trip to Io. Only Tom's quick thinking and careful handling of their small lander craft had enabled the young people to land on Io, discover the alien probe, and return to the *Daniel Boone* safely. The lieutenant's flagrant violation of his commanding officer's orders had resulted in a court-martial, a fact which added to the young officer's personal hatred of Tom and everyone who was connected with Swift Enterprises.

"He was court-martialed, but he was paroled," Tom explained. "As a favor to the navy, Dad agreed Foster could be assigned to the naval installation on the far side of Triton dome. He was to be kept under careful watch. I guess the watch wasn't careful enough," he added ruefully.

"We'd better catch him before he takes the probe out of Triton," Ben said.

"I'll alert security." Tom moved to the computer and punched a sequence of buttons. Swiftly he explained to the answering officers what had happened and asked that a full alert be declared until Foster was located.

"Let's go chase the guy," Ben urged when Tom had finished his conversation.

"It would be better if we stayed here for the next few minutes," Tom countered. "We have no idea which way Foster ran. Triton is a huge place. He could be going in any of a dozen ways or hiding in scores of places. Security can cover the entire undersea city faster than we could even begin hunting. If we remain here, they'll know where to get us. Besides," he added, surveying the ruined lab, "it might be a better idea to look around for any clues Foster might have left."

"You're right," Anita put in as she began to go through the debris on one of the work tables.

"It is all my fault," Aristotle said in his distinctive voice. "I am a flawed mechanism. That becomes more and more evident. I was inadequate to prevent the abduction of Aracta."

"Aracta? Who's Aracta?" Tom demanded.

"The alien intelligence," Aristotle replied. "I only found out its name a very short time ago. I thought I had made a breakthrough and that is when I came to your lab, Tom, to report to you, when the general security alarm sounded and—"

"Aristotle," Ben said, "take it chronologically."

"Aracta and I were discussing the social history of the human race—"

"You were chatting with it?" Ben asked, incredulously.

"Yes, Ben. As I said, I achieved a breakthrough shortly after you went to bed last night. Aracta has been understandably cautious. After all, we may not be the sort of help the Skree need."

"We?" Anita asked, anxiously.

"Swift Enterprises," Aristotle replied. "You know the Skree built and sent out Aracta to get needed help. Actually, they delegated 192 probes toward Class G stars with planetary bodies."

"The aliens need the same sort of sun we do," said Tom. "The probe said it came from Alpha Centauri. That's a Class G star."

"Yes," said Aristotle. "And the Skree desperately need assistance, but they do not want to give the secret of the stardrive to just anyone."

"You mentioned a breakthrough in communications," Tom said, bringing the subject back.

"Correct. Aracta and I were exchanging histories of the races that created us. We were communicating, I'm afraid, at a speed your senses could not achieve."

"Don't apologize," Tom said with some irritation.

Aristotle quickly told Anita and Ben about his recent discovery that the probe was severely malfunctioning in some areas.

"I am still searching my memory and trying to correlate certain facts and theories. It is possible that Foster was aiding in Aracta's escape."

"Escape?" Anita asked, incredulous.

"Alas, yes." Aristotle said. "What I had come to tell you, Tom, in addition to the information I had time to convey before the general alarm was sounded, was that Aracta has understood what you, Anita, Ben, and Foster have been saying for quite some time. It used me as camouflage."

"You mean it picked your memory when you weren't aware of it and learned our language?" asked Tom.

"Yes," answered the robot. "It had already started on Io."

"That long ago!" exclaimed Ben.

"I now remember a certain statement that the lieutenant made just before you ordered him back to the ship while we were on Io," the mechanoid continued. "He said, 'If we can analyze the probe's stardrive, we will have the secret of interstellar travel. *We could build the mightiest army in the galaxy!*' That last phrase is the key, Tom. A powerful army is what the Skree need. Foster seems to have offered that."

"So Foster can talk to it?" Tom said with tight lips. "He knows that the alien is armed and dangerous?"

"He is aware of the weaponry capabilities of Aracta. I am sorry. I should have made the connection between the lieutenant's phrase on Io and the mission of Aracta as soon as I became aware that Aracta had learned our language. I have failed again," concluded the mechanoid sorrowfully.

Before anyone could respond, the computer chimed and the wallscreen flashed on. A head shot of Sergeant Garrott filled the screen.

"I have some bad news," the security officer announced. "Lieutenant Foster has escaped from Triton!"

# Chapter Three

"Escaped!" the young people chorused in dismay.

"How?" Tom demanded.

"He boarded the *Jose Arias Espinoza,* a luxury-class submarine yacht which he rented from Triton Marine Rentals at fourteen hundred hours yesterday on Dock Ten."

"Why wasn't he stopped?" Tom cried.

"A masterful job had been done on our general alarm system," the sergeant replied. "Someone had jammed only selected sections of the alarm and security systems, and those sections were made inoperative for only selected times.

Whoever did it had planned everything very carefully. The system was tampered with just enough to foul everything up, but not enough to set off any of the internal warning devices."

"Aracta must have done it," Aristotle said.

"Sergeant, we've got to go after Foster," Tom snapped. "Please clear the fastest sub available. We're going to the dock area immediately."

"Okay, Tom," the sergeant replied.

"Come on," the young inventor said to the other three in the lab. "We've got to catch Foster and the probe."

The four set off for the dock area at a rapid clip. As they turned a bend in the corridor, they ran into Colonel Pascal, chief of security for Triton dome.

"Hey, young fella," the colonel sputtered at Tom, "where do you think you're going so fast?"

"Emergency, Colonel," Tom replied. "You should check with Sergeant Garrott. I'm surprised he hasn't called you. We've got a crisis on our hands!"

The young man opened a red door marked RESTRICTED ACCESS and began to step through.

"Stop!" the security chief shouted. "You can't go in there!"

"*Colonel*! They're escaping. Lieutenant Foster

and the alien probe—they're getting away!" Tom attempted to explain while the other three scampered through the doorway and down toward the docks.

"What alien probe? Foster—he's navy, isn't he? What's the navy got to do with this?"

"No time to explain. Call your office," Tom suggested as he dived after his friends.

The older man looked at the red door for a moment. A lot of fuss, he thought to himself. Maybe the Luna Corporation might like to hear about this. It was just the sort of thing for which they paid him a little extra. Being a minority stockholder in Triton, they had a perfect right to know what was going on behind the scenes. "Especially with the Swifts," was the way it had been put to him.

Nothing was wrong with making a buck on the side, Pascal thought. Just doing my duty. He punched out a code on his private communicator, then waited for an answer.

Tom and his friends certainly had been upset about something, hadn't they?

Sergeant Garrott was waiting for the young people at the entrance to the docks. Tom skidded to a halt beside him. "Got it?" he asked.

"Yes. The fastest sub available. It's on Slip Sixteen."

"Thanks," the young man replied. "Please keep us posted on any new information about either Foster or my father's condition." Tom hated to leave without knowing more about Mr. Swift's injuries but he realized the older man was receiving the best medical care possible. Besides, nothing would speed his father's recovery faster than knowing the probe had been returned to Swift Enterprises.

The four passengers ran down the metal corridor toward the hive of submarine docking areas.

It was colder here, at the outer skin of Triton, and wetter. They ran past sealed and open hatches containing a variety of vessels. Some were company subs used for inspection and seafarming. Others were private yachts in from Jamaica, Miami, and the Bahamas. A few were research vessels capable of descending to the depths of the Puerto Rican Trench or the Yucatan Basin. There were also gaily painted submarines of treasure hunters who roamed the ancient shipping lanes of the Spanish galleons hauling gold and treasure out of Mexico.

The larger cargo ships were berthed farther

along. These massive vessels were of two kinds: the general-purpose cargo sub and the semi-sub, consisting mostly of living quarters and giant nuclear engines. These powerful tugs could haul two or three streamlined, unmanned trailers through the oceans of the world, delivering cargo to commercial ports.

But it was into a fast racer that Tom and his friends descended. Getting through the hatch into the interior was a tight fit for Aristotle. By the time all the hatches were cycled shut and sealed, Tom was in the control seat, requesting clearance.

"Find out which way they went," he said to Anita as she slipped into the copilot's seat.

Then he turned his attention to getting the sleek, tapering vessel out of its berth and into the lock.

By the time they had cleared, the port authority sonar had verified that the *Jose Arias Espinoza* was traveling north-northeast at top speed.

Ben frowned as he looked over Tom's shoulder at the map displayed on the screen. "Newfoundland?"

"Foster could zigzag around that and go to Greenland or Iceland," Anita said, studying the

map. "Or go east to England, up to Russia . . ." Her voice trailed off. "There's a lot of ocean."

"And a lot of mixed currents," Tom said, frowning. "He could be laying a false trail. Once out of sonar range he could go south and swing toward Africa."

"Tom, that's a *lot* of territory," Ben protested. "We could lose him, easily."

"Aristotle," Tom called out. "Have you any suggestions?"

"I am reviewing the profile on Lieutenant Foster now, Tom. I think your best plan would be to track him through his mind rather than through the ocean."

Ben laughed. "Oh, great. I may be a full-blooded Cherokee Indian, but even I can't see footprints on the mind!"

"Aristotle's right," Tom responded. "Foster is probably laying a false trail. He's heading out to sea where he has room and where there are none of Swift Enterprises' sonar tracking stations."

"Plenty of other ones, though," Anita reminded the young inventor. She reached out and tapped a section of the control panel before them. "They've all got them. Every yacht, cargo sub, military vessel, surface ship, playtime skid,

deepsea digger, oil rig—everything."

"And the sea is full of ships!" Ben said happily. "All kinds of sea lanes run through this part of the Atlantic, under the ocean as well as on top."

"But Foster knows that," Tom insisted. "Aristotle, what is the range of the *Espinoza*?"

"About 2,000 miles, at present nuclear fuel capacity."

"You checked with the rental company?" Ben asked.

"Correct. As to diving capacity, 15,000 feet is the maximum with a safety recommendation of 12,000. The basins in the Caribbean are as deep as 16,400 feet, if the *Espinoza* should turn back that way. The average depth of the Atlantic is approximately 11,000 feet, but the South Sandwich Trench goes down to 30,000. That is, of course, in the South Atlantic."

"And to the northwest?" Anita asked.

"I believe the *Espinoza* is capable of descending to almost any depth needed," Aristotle replied.

"So they can hide anywhere," Ben muttered.

"Anita—put out the word. Alert the United States Navy and the Royal Navy to be on the

lookout. And then, please check if there has been any change in my father's condition."

She noticed the strain on Tom's face when she reached for the headset. He was looking out of the thick glassite port at the clear Bahamian water. Schools of fish darted out of the way. A cargo sub, painted in the yellow and red colors of maritime merchants, slipped by below them. They passed the stringer buoys marking off a seafarm area where an enormous herd of fish was kept out of the sealanes by a sonic fence.

"Your father is conscious, Tom," Anita reported after a few minutes. "The doctors say he'll have a headache for a while, but he'll be okay."

Tom was relieved and smiled weakly at his friends. "That's good to hear. Now let's go over this thing with Foster. We know he was in some kind of communication with the alien . . . uh . . . with Aracta." Tom looked at Aristotle, a quizzical expression on his face. "I confess I find it odd to have gender designation for robots. I think of you as a 'he' because of your personality and your name. But is Aracta a he, a she, or an it? Or doesn't it matter?" he added with a grin.

"I confess, Tom, that gender is a mystery to me. I understand it biologically and logically, accepting life forms for what they are. But gender in human beings seems to dictate personality to some extent."

"So does environment and experience," Anita put in quickly.

"What term do we use with Aracta?" Ben asked.

"The simplest would be he, I think," the squat robot replied. "It has to do with original programing, which was done by beings closely resembling the male gender in *homo sapiens*. May I remind you that it was a male human who programed me?"

Tom chuckled.

"I didn't think specifically of giving you a male orientation," he said, shaking his head. "It must have been subconscious."

"So much of the prejudice in this world is," Anita remarked. "But let's get back to Foster and Aracta. Aristotle, you said you didn't think Aracta was stolen. Do you mean he cooperated?"

"That is a possibility," Aristotle said. "While I was teaching Aracta terran languages, he was teaching me the Skree language. Language—at least on Earth—is a solemn indicator of attitude. The Skree, and thus Aracta, are somewhat suspicious and fearful. But then, they have a right to be. They have been beset by warlike races almost from the beginning of their history."

Aristotle paused for a minute. "It is possible that Aracta's actions may be my fault. I did not delete the history of human warfare from what I communicated to him."

"You did right," Tom said. "Show them the bad as well as the good."

"Evidently, what came through to him is the success of organized armies in our warfare."

"The military aspects," said Ben. "Of course, Foster would appeal to that angle. He's a military man with a military mind. Does the probe know Foster was court-martialed?"

"He did once, but as we discovered during our return trip to Earth, Ben, Aracta is not functioning with a complete memory. It is in the memory that the inhibitions are contained."

"You mean Aracta isn't playing with a full deck," Ben said.

"If I understand your vernacular statement—yes. But the probe is very quick. We started talking quite logically with binary, but once we established a suitable route of communication, we proceeded quickly."

"As only robots can," muttered Anita.

"Aracta outlined the difficulties of the Skree

race and stated that if a suitable commitment was forthcoming, he was prepared to give us the technological information necessary to construct a stardrive. I believe Foster has deliberately misled Aracta."

There was silence in the cabin. What a carrot to dangle! thought Tom. Instead of the years, even centuries, necessary to travel to the nearest stars, they might get there in months, or weeks, or *even less*! Who could know how time functions outside the normal time-space universe? It might be an infinity or no time at all.

*Stardrive!* Almost anything was worth that. No wonder a ruthless man would be tempted to break the law for it.

"Sergeant Garrott is calling from Triton," Anita interrupted Tom's thoughts. "I'll put him on the speakers."

"Hello, Tom. We've reconstructed what happened in your father's lab by replaying the surveillance cameras which were automatically activated when Foster forced his way in while your father was out.

"Foster went immediately to the computer and began programing sequences which apparently had been written on a piece of paper he had with him. The cameras did not give a clear picture of the paper, so we're not sure about that, but Foster kept referring to it. Now we realize that he was jamming much of our equipment." The security officer looked at a pad in front of him, then continued.

"He must have known your father would bring the probe to his private lab because he hid after finishing his work on the computer."

Ben muttered under his breath and Anita realized this information was making Tom very upset.

"When your father entered the lab," the man went on, "Foster jumped him immediately. They struggled for several minutes. Your father put up quite a fight, Tom, but then he slipped, knocking his head against a heavy lab table as he went down. That's what knocked him out."

"Thanks, Sergeant," Tom said. "We really appreciate your letting us know."

"Wait, there's more. I don't know how to explain this, but the probe was in communication with someone or something outside the laboratory."

"What!" Tom exclaimed while Ben and Anita looked at each other in amazement.

"For some reason, right after Foster took the probe from your father, he connected it to the computer in the lab. It used a commercial channel and a library channel. He did it quite openly without even bothering to jam the frequencies."

There was silence in the crowded cabin for a few minutes, then Tom nodded. "Thanks, Sergeant Garrott. Please keep in touch."

"You bet," the officer replied. "And—good luck!"

The color of the sea had darkened around the ship, indicating a greater depth. There were fewer fish, but the submarine's sonar registered a number of passing surface ships and undersea vessels. A spherical deepsea mining sub appeared on the scope ahead and they passed over it as it began to rise slowly.

Ahead of them the *Espinoza* continued on its mysterious course, moving at the same speed, with Tom and his crew following.

"There's another point to consider," Tom spoke up. "Foster is mentally unbalanced as well. Aracta may think *him* sane and the rest of us crazy."

"Because Aracta is mad, you mean?" Anita asked.

Tom nodded ruefully.

"I have an opinion to offer," Aristotle said.

"This is only an opinion. It is difficult to understand truly alien thinking when you know only human thought processes."

"My father was finding that out with his dolphin research," Tom said. "But go on—anything might help at this stage."

"It was nothing Aracta said," the robot continued. "It might be in what he did not say!"

# Chapter Four

Ben, Tom, and Anita stared at the robot in surprise.

"What do you mean?" Tom asked.

"I think Aracta felt vulnerable," Aristotle said. "From his beginning he was surrounded by the exo-skeleton of his ship, which had considerable weapons and sensing devices."

"So he felt helpless?" Tom asked quickly. "Captured by beings he thought might be the enemy and exposed, he feared for his survival?"

"Aracta's sole consideration was the successful completion of his mission," Aristotle said. "His continued existence was of secondary importance to that of the primary mission."

"But why go with Foster?" Anita asked. "What could he do for Aracta that we couldn't?"

"Foster must have had help," Tom said seriously. "Yet very few people knew what we found on Io. The alien's existence was kept secret from even the crew of the *Daniel Boone.*"

"Captain Barrot knew, we knew, Foster, who else?" Ben asked.

"Foster must have talked to someone," Anita declared. She turned to Aristotle. "Check with Triton communications and see if Foster called out and to whom."

"Checking," the robot replied.

Tom stared out the porthole at the dark sea. "After Foster was court-martialed on the *Boone,* while we were coming back, he swore he'd get even. He blamed me—all of us, actually—for his mistakes and his disgrace."

"I thought Captain Barrot was very lenient," Anita said. "He was simply transferred to Earthside duty and ordered to undergo psychiatric examination."

"Yes, but that's a terrible thing for a career officer," Tom said. "It's in his record and he'll probably not rise in rank and end up running a desk in some out-of-the-way base."

"And never get back into space," Ben added softly. "For all his faults, Foster did like being in space."

"So, faced with a dead-end career, he chose to try something else," Anita said. "And being a little bit crazy, he chose a crazy scheme."

"Pardon me," Aristotle said. "Lieutenant Foster only made four calls out of the dome. Three were military in nature: filing an appeal to his court-martial, a request for transfer, and a call to a Commander Pournelle at the Space Forces base in Mojave."

"And the other?" Anita asked.

"To David Luna, President of the Luna Corporation."

Ben and Tom whistled.

"Luna runs most of the mining operations on the Moon," Ben said thoughtfully.

Tom sighed. "If you were to take all the robber barons in the world and roll them into one, and add a dash of corrupt political connections, you'd have David Luna. But he's not an easy man to get hold of. I wonder how Foster actually got through to him?"

"He had special information," Ben said. "How long was the call, Aristotle?"

"One hour, twenty-nine minutes."

"*Very* expensive," Anita said. "But long enough to work through secretaries and all those people hired to filter out crank calls and time-wasters."

"Algeria!" Tom said suddenly. "The Luna Corporation has the largest private spaceport in the world in the Sahara, south of Biskra."

"Of course!" Ben exclaimed, snapping his fingers. "Foster is heading toward Casablanca! Then a quick flight over the Atlas Mountains to the Sahara spaceport!"

"Into space?" asked Anita. "But why? Luna must have huge labs here on Earth."

"Why did we take Aracta to Triton?" Tom explained. "For secrecy. Well, on the Moon or out in the asteroids—which Luna is just beginning to exploit—there would be total security."

"He could be going to Poseidon. That's the new undersea dome near the Azores," Ben suggested. I remember reading that the Luna Corporation had an interest in it."

"Uh-oh," Tom said in a voice that got the attention of the others. "The Luna Corporation bought a chunk of Triton last year.. Not enough to scare us. It wasn't a take-over bid, but enough to get a foothold. And Luna bought a piece of the Nereid dome a few months back."

"That's the recreational dome near the Canary Islands, isn't it?" Ben asked, and Tom nodded. "So we've got three possibilities—two undersea ports where Foster's sub could berth with no trouble . . . and Casablanca."

"If we take the time to search the domes and he goes to Casablanca—" Anita said, shrugging.

Tom's attention was caught by a movement on the sonar screen. "He's changing direction!"

They all bent over the screen. "He's circling!" Ben exclaimed. "Let's move to cut him off!"

"No, look, he's diving," Tom observed. "And deeply!"

They watched as Foster's sub spiraled down, swinging farther south, and descending into the Hatteras Abyssal Plain, the eastern edge of the North American continent.

"What's he up to?" Anita muttered. They kept a close watch on the depth and pressure gauges as their sub followed.

"Just evasion tactics," Ben suggested.

For an hour they followed Foster intently, going south again, and descending constantly.

Then Foster leveled off and took an erratic course near the sea bottom. The floor of the ocean rose slowly as they drew toward Cuba and Haiti, still some distance away.

Tom flashed the coast and geodetic survey maps on the computer screen. In this area there was only the most basic information—current direction and a rough map of the ocean floor, much like a long-distance photo with only the largest features recorded.

Then, without warning, Foster's sub disappeared from the sonar image!

"Hey—wait a minute!" Ben exclaimed. He rescanned the area, narrowing the focus, but the sub had simply disappeared.

They stared at the ghostly green ripples of bottom sand and the upthrust shelves of submarine rock. Their sub came closer to the last recorded site, but they saw nothing except the undersea floor on their screens.

"What's that?" Anita said, pointing out of the porthole into the dark water that was almost devoid of sea life at this depth.

A spiny shape appeared ahead, just faintly visible. Tom focused the sonar and the image of something roughly crescent-shaped firmed up.

"It's a ship!" Ben exclaimed. His finger

touched the surface of the screen. "Look, it has the high back typical of a galleon—a Spanish galleon!"

"A sunken ship!" Anita said.

"Never mind that," Tom said. "Where's Foster?"

The vessel lay tilted on its side on a shelf of rock. A cliff, twice as high as the broken masts of the galleon, rose above it.

They passed the wreck at some distance, seeing it better now. It seemed in remarkably good condition.

"Why isn't it all broken up and covered with sea life?" Anita wondered.

"Probably because this far down the water is extremely cold and relatively undisturbed. Most of the microscopic organisms that would eat into the wood prefer to live in warmer temperatures," Tom explained.

As they passed the wreck, their sonar continued to detect nothing ahead, so Tom turned the small sub around.

"Foster couldn't have simply disappeared," he insisted. "There must be a logical explanation. The only unique thing back there was the galleon. Let's go back and take a closer look."

Anita and Ben shrugged. "Suits me," Ben said. "Besides, I have no other suggestions."

The galleon grew on the screen, barely noticeable against the cliff behind it. They stopped twenty yards away and shone a spotlight over it.

The ship had lost both masts, probably in a storm, and shards of rigging still clung in tangled clumps to the tilted deck. The hull had ruptured, breaking the ship almost in two, probably as a result of landing on the shelf or on the cliff above and falling to the shelf below.

"Wait a minute," Tom said. He swung the spotlight to the ripped hull. From this angle the crack was only about six feet high, not much larger than a half-opened door. Something glittered in the darkness beyond. Tom moved the sub closer and slightly to the starboard. Anita gasped aloud.

"Gold!" she exclaimed.

It was beautiful, untarnished gold. They saw a life-sized head and bust with a feathered headdress and precious stones for eyes. A standing figure of a warrior over two feet high. A mask, a jaguar, some kind of pot. A collection of staffs and ritual spears tied with the rotting remnant of a leather strap. All solid gold.

"An oxygen tank! Look—" Ben pointed urgently.

Amid the neatly stacked golden treasure was a single tank, blue straps waving slowly in the motion caused by the sub.

"Someone's been here," Anita cried.

"Or *is* here," Tom muttered. He quickly moved the light back and forth over the ship, then back to the rotting hold. Beyond he could dimly see more treasures, glints of gold, the sparkle of a red jewel.

"I believe I have identified the vessel," Aristotle said. "It corresponds to a description in the records at Madrid, at least from superficial examination. It is probably the treasure galleon *El Testigo Santo,* Captain Geraldo Jamarillo commanding. It set sail from Mexico on June 2, 1523, laden with tribute from the city of Teotihuacan, now known as Mexico City. It had been foretold that Topiltzin, or Quetzalcoatl, the priest-king of Tula who had left his people, would someday return from the east in the year One Reed, which falls every fifty-two years in the Mesoamerican calendar. In 1519 Hernando Cortes set sail for Mexico."

"And landed in the year One Reed," finished Tom. "This is part of his loot, then?"

"The exact origin of this cargo is unknown, but it seems likely, Tom."

"And someone found it," Anita sighed.

"Foster?" Ben asked. "No, this is not his sort of thing. He's a space type."

"But David Luna has many interests," Tom said. "However, that still doesn't explain Foster's disappearance."

"Why don't we look on the other side near the cliff?" Ben suggested.

"Good idea," Tom agreed. He brought the sub up, and Anita sighed again as the golden cargo passed from sight.

"So pretty," she commented.

"And valuable," Ben said. "More for historical reasons than gold content—oh-oh!" he interrupted himself.

The sub had drifted up over the tilted deck. Tom's spotlight illuminated the rotting wood and was now probing at the base of the cliff. It was black there. They should have seen the cliff itself.

"A cave," Ben whispered. "Big enough to take the *Espinoza.*"

"Maybe they're waiting for us," Anita warned.

Tom halted the sub, steadying it in front of the cave mouth. His spotlight found the edges of the cave, but it was as dark as a tomb. The sonar could not bring out any distinct images, separating them from the walls.

"Do we go in?" Ben asked.

"Let's wait," Anita said. "They can't stay there forever."

"Neither can we. Why don't we call for help and have someone stake out the place?" Ben suggested.

Tom rubbed his chin in thought. The racing sub they had was not equipped with deep diving equipment. Its single virtue was speed. With three humans aboard plus a large robot it was very crowded. There was only so much food and air. They couldn't wait.

"I'm going in!" Tom declared.

# Chapter Five

"Hey, you mean *we're* going in!" Ben amended.

The sub slowly nosed into the cave. Tom had his hands on the controls, ready to back out at a moment's notice.

Something glittered ahead. More gold.

Part of the ship's cargo had evidently been transferred to the cave and laid out in a row along the righthand wall. Three thick, crudely cast bars of gold. A squat figure in a fan-shaped headdress. A white plastic box spilling out armbands, necklaces, loose emeralds, and a few golden pins. A rather plain statue which bore some vicious cuts as if someone had hacked at the soft metal with an axe.

A second treasure, Tom thought, enough to start a museum.

Visions of the exotic Aztec empire came to Tom's mind. Half-buried jungle cities, blood sacrifices, massive heads carved from boulders, delicate ceramic figurines. Great stone pyramids, tiered and ramped, capped with once-bloody altar stones. But beyond the rites that seemed savage and cruel to contemporary eyes, the Aztecs—as well as the Mayans, Incas, the Toltecs, and others—had had civilizations amazingly advanced, quite complex and sophisticated.

"I'm sure David Luna's outfit worked on this," Ben said, interrupting his friend's daydreams. "They're big on submarine research."

"And on exploitation," Anita added. "These statues may just pop up for sale, one by one, without any archeological research."

Tom nodded, "You're probably right. But now the show's over. We came in here to find Foster."

Ben grinned. "Hey, it isn't every day you see anything like this!"

"I know. This is a fantastic find. But the one we made on Io is more important and—"

"Look out!" Anita yelled suddenly.

The *Espinoza* shot out of the darkness like an attacking shark. Anita screamed as the two subs sideswiped each other. A great ringing gong shook them all as metal struck metal. Alarm lights blinked on, a loud klaxon deafened everyone. The entire ship shuddered.

Then the *Espinoza* passed, escaping through the mouth of the cave.

Tom shook his head and checked Damage Control. The hull was intact, but several dials were edging into their red emergency indicators. Carefully, he backed the racer out of the cave. It was tight between the cave mouth and the wrecked galleon, but Tom switched on the rear television cameras—and jumped with surprise!

"Look!" he pointed.

The *Espinoza* had rammed into the galleon, stabbing through it like a sharp knife. But the ship was caught in the thick timbers of the hull. Its rear elevators were jammed and the screw churned up the water. Bubbles were rising in enormous silver clouds from the damaged port side.

"He's sinking!" Anita yelled.

"We've got to free him so he can get to the surface!" Tom exclaimed. He moved closer to the trapped vessel and carefully nosed his racing sub into a space between Foster's ship and the shattered hull of the treasure galleon.

"You'll wreck the galleon!" Ben warned. "It'll fall off the shelf and all the treasure will be scattered!"

"And if I don't," Tom said grimly, "Foster'll sink!"

He revved up the powerful engines of the sub, then drove the vessel into the galleon, wrenching the stout but ancient timbers apart. The sub shuddered and scraped against Foster's ship. The silt of centuries shifted down from above them, murking the water and making it almost impossible to see. A falling timber thunked against the hull.

They heard the screech of the ancient Spanish ship as Tom literally pried it apart. There was a metallic clang and a rasping along the hull, then Foster's submarine pulled free.

"He's getting out!" Ben exclaimed.

There was a creaking moan and a crash which echoed through the vessel, as though a giant was beating on the hull with a mighty hammer. Tom reversed the engines and tried to pull away, but he only managed to back up a few feet before they came to a groaning stop.

The *El Testigo Santo* had collapsed around them. They were trapped!

"Check the hull," Tom ordered. He shut down the twin screws of the ship, bringing an eerie silence to the craft.

"Okay," Ben said, turning to squeeze past Aristotle. There was not much room, as the racer had been built to use a small crew.

Tom examined the read-outs on fuel, air pressure, and other vital statistics while Anita tried to see out the portholes that were obscured by the dislodged silt. Aristotle remained silent and unmoving as he always did when he had no physical work to do. But that did not mean he was not thinking.

"Everything is okay back here," Ben shouted from the next compartment. "No water. But a couple of big timbers are wedged against the elevators. I can see that much through the port here."

The water outside was still churning and smokelike silt obscured vision in every direction. Anita turned to Tom, concern on her face. "Are we trapped?"

The young inventor nodded. "Yes—at least temporarily." He pointed at the dials. "But we have a reasonable enough air supply."

"What do you figure as reasonable?" Ben asked as he wedged himself back into the small control room.

"Thirteen hours. Maybe fourteen."

"Thirteen point two," Aristotle confirmed. "At present rate of consumption, that is."

"Okay," Tom said. He was not about to argue that sort of thing with a precise mind like Aristotle's. "But this isn't like being out in space. All we have to do is surface and breathe that gorgeous Caribbean air."

"Tom, it might as well be space," Ben said. "If we can't get to it, we can't breathe it."

"Let's try going forward," Anita said. "If backwards is blocked . . ."

Tom nodded and started up the engines again. The powerful screws shoved the submarine ahead a few feet as the terrible screeching of the timbers resumed. More silt cascaded down from the deck over their heads. A corroded block from the rigging fell outside a port. Then there was a loud thump over their heads and a thick, curved rib, as thick as a man's torso, slid over the front ports and wedged tightly. Tom increased the thrust, but the timber stayed put. He reversed the engines and tried to pull back, letting the stout rib fall before them; however, they found themselves wedged tighter than ever.

Then they heard the groan.

It was an eerie sound, half-human, almost a shriek. The sound increased in volume and they felt two more thumps on their metal hull. The submarine started to tilt.

"Look out!" cried Anita. "We're turning over!"

"The galleon is going over the cliff!" Ben shouted.

Tom's fingers stabbed at the submarine's electronic controls, driving the twin screws to their utmost. They were not prepared for the sudden tipping. Only Tom had his seat belt on. Anita had loosened hers to get a better view out the portholes. Aristotle put out his two arms and braced his weight against the hull. But it was Ben who suffered the most. Trapped between the control seats and Aristotle, he fell one way, then tumbled as the submarine turned completely over.

Objects all over the undersea vessel rained from their compartments, crashing and shattering. Most things on the submarine were fastened down, but the designers of the craft had not anticipated a somersault.

Tom braced himself, trying to see what was happening through the storms of mud and silt. The Spanish galleon had obviously been moved first by the ramming of Foster's ship. Then, by the violent wrenchings of Tom's vessel, it had been shoved off the ledge.

Their racer was falling into the abyss along with the old treasure ship!

They stopped tumbling and suddenly there was a kind of strange silence, broken only by a faint creaking.

They were gliding serenely into the depths far beyond the rated capabilities of the small sub. Soon they would be crushed by the pressure.

Frantically, Tom pumped power into the engines, driving forward, then backward, then forward again, rocking the galleon which trapped them. He didn't know how far they might fall, but if they hit the bottom with the weight of the galleon still around them, they would be killed. Even if the water pressure did not crush them, the effect of crashing with the treasure ship on top of them would certainly squash them.

A golden idol struck the thick glassite of the front port, leered at them for a second, and fell away as Tom reversed the engines.

Suddenly there was a creak, then a moan.

Without warning the Spanish wreck was cascading past them. They were free!

Ben and Anita let out a shout as the racer backed away from the ancient timbers. The water cleared after a few minutes and Ben crawled back to check out the inner hull.

They popped out into a bright afternoon. A metal-vaned schooner was passing by, its computer-controlled sails a series of panels which could be aimed toward or away from the wind. A sailor on deck waved as Anita opened the outer hatch and took a deep breath of tangy, salty air. The redhead waved back, then started the air compressors.

They all came together in the control room. "We'll be topped off in a few minutes," Ben said. "But where is Foster?"

"We lost him," Tom said, disappointed. "He's not on sonar, or rather, he could be any of those blips. Which one do we chase?"

"Some are cargo subs," Anita said. "Maybe a few pleasure crafts, but . . ." She sighed. "You're right, which one?" She looked at Tom wearily. "That's what we get for saving his life!"

"His hull leak must not have been as bad as it seemed," Ben suggested. "Or else he was willing to take a big risk just to get away from us." The

Cherokee computer expert frowned. "Well, what now?"

"Close the hatch," Tom ordered. Anita pressed the stud that activated the outer hatch, but her eyebrows went up questioningly.

Tom's fingers worked rapidly over the keyboard of the navigation computer. Then he punched the course in, and they felt the submarine swing around.

"We're not going north . . . *or* east to Casablanca!" Anita exclaimed in surprise. "We're going south?"

"Oh, I get it," Ben said. "We're going to swing back, put in at the Bahamas, and *fly* to . . . to where?"

"Casablanca," Tom said. "Once Luna has the probe off Earth, out of effective legal range, he can do anything he wants. Foster will try to leave Earth as fast as possible."

Tom set the autopilot and stood up in the cramped cabin. "I suggest we get some sleep, even if it's only for an hour or two." He looked at Anita and said, "After being out in space for as long as we were, this full gravity must be pretty tiring for you."

Anger flushed Anita's face. "I'll make it, Tom

Swift, even if I did spend most of my life on a space colony!"

This flash of Anita's old resentment surprised Tom. He had not meant his remark to be patronizing. He was tired after months of much less gravity or no gravity at all. He decided not to try and explain himself; it would probably only make the situation worse.

They began hooking up the mesh hammocks. Ben rolled into his with a grateful sigh, murmuring to the robot, "Aristotle, ol' buddy, keep a watch out for sea monsters and pirates."

"Science has shown that those creatures thought to be sea monsters were, in reality—"

"Aristotle, he's kidding," Anita said rather sharply.

"Oh," the robot replied. "I'll never understand imprecise human language and the tendency to exaggeration or untruth for a humorous effect."

"Um," Ben said, sleepily.

"Stand watch," Tom said.

"Yes, Tom," Aristotle responded. He stood, immobile and silent, his lenses fixed upon the control panel and at the view of the seabed he could see ahead.

# Chapter Six

Tom, Anita, and Ben walked swiftly through the sleek concrete arches of the new Filali Airport outside Casablanca. Aristotle rolled along behind them using the convenient wheels beneath his feet.

The new Free Passage Act had eliminated the time-consuming customs search, so they immediately flagged an electro-taxi at the curb.

"Aristotle," Tom said, pointing, "you follow us."

"Yes, Tom."



"The Port Captain's office," Ben told the driver, who was eyeing Aristotle with some fear. Anthropoid robots were new in this part of the world and he was not sure what to make of the large mechanoid, even if it did seem to ignore him. The driver put his taxi in gear and it hummed out from the curb, pulling into traffic.

Aristotle rolled along behind, drawing lots of stares and open-mouthed amazement from the robed Moroccans. Anita stifled a laugh at the reaction of one young man, who almost fell from his bicycle.

"I don't think they've seen too many robots around here," she giggled, her good humor restored by some sleep.

"How's he doing?" Tom asked Ben, who was looking out the back window.

"Showing off. He's going around the potholes on one foot."

"Well, we did give him the option of wheels or feet, depending on which worked best," Tom chuckled.

The Port Captain's office was chaotic. No one seemed to be in charge and it required Aristotle to translate Tom's English into an official's French. They were told Foster's submarine had docked an hour earlier.

"Back to the airport!" Tom cried, and they raced out into the bright, hot sun. As they tumbled into the electro-taxi of another startled driver, Tom called to Aristotle, "Contact the airport! Get us a Blackhawk jet if one's available! If there are any questions, ask them to call Swift Enterprises in Shopton! Have someone waiting for us!"

"Yes, Tom," the robot replied. With his internal radio the amazing mechanoid called the airport by sending a signal to one of the synchronous satellites in orbit over North Africa—going over 45,000 miles just to call someone ten miles ahead.

When the lumbering electro-cab arrived, a maintenance crew was wheeling out a sleek Blackhawk, a small private jet favored by corporation executives whose time was more valuable than money.

Minutes later, the English pilot lifted the ship off smoothly, heading northwest over the rugged Atlas Mountains toward the sprawling Sahara Base.

"He's ahead of us again," Ben grumbled. "They must have had everything set up and ready to go."

Tom nodded. "But we were right—Foster did

sail here. That rich man's yacht he leased was pretty fast."

"I just hope we don't turn out to be a day late and a dollar short," Ben remarked gloomily.

"If Sahara Base belongs to Luna, won't he be expecting us?" Anita asked.

"I suppose so. He must have some sort of spy system in Triton alerting him to what's going on. We have to assume he knows we are after Foster."

"So they'll try to stop us?" Ben asked, glowering around. "Maybe the pilot is in on it and is taking us somewhere else."

"I have been monitoring the flight by satellite transmission, Ben, and the pilot is taking us to the Sahara Base," Aristotle spoke up.

"But what do we do when we land?" Anita asked. "That place is huge! He leases launch space to a number of companies and countries, doesn't he? Where do we even begin to look? They might send Foster up in some freighter flying a Liberian flag, a Luna Corporation ship, smuggled on board a National Geographic Survey, even a Pan-Luna commercial flight."

Tom chewed his lip a moment. "They'll have everything set up to go. That's the way it has been so far. So we look for the next ship out."

He turned to Aristotle. "Call Swift Enterprises again. Have them go to Priority Red on this—get us some kind of transportation. Check with *New America.* See if the Luna Corporation has a ship there ready to go to the moon or to the asteroid belt."

"Good thinking," Ben said.

"Have *New America* ready the fastest ship that Swift Enterprises has there with fuel and provision for a flight as far away as the asteroids and back."

"You think he's going there?" Anita asked.

"Better we're prepared for the longer flight," Tom replied. "Aristotle, have *New America* put tight security on whatever ship they pick for us."

"Yes, Tom. Transmitting."

"Touchdown in ten minutes," the pilot's voice came over the intercom from the control deck.

Tom, Ben, and Anita exchanged looks. Where would their chase lead?

As Tom buckled himself in for the landing, he wondered how his father was and wished he could ask for the older man's advice. To lose a stardrive would be disastrous, but to have it fall into the hands of someone as ruthless and unscrupulous as David Luna would be even worse. If Luna were to control the expansion of mankind into the stars, there was no telling what might happen.

And he would stop at nothing—not even killing—to get the secret of the stardrive.

They *had* to retrieve the Skree probe with its all-important message!

Biskra baked in the sun, an incongruous grouping of stone houses, metallic domes, donkeys, tall spindly masts, camels, dust, veiled women, and the distant roar of great rockets thrusting into the sky. There were strong men in form-fitting jumpers with the insignia of large corporations, animal droppings, and myriad odors of rotting garbage, exotic cooking, ozone, and sweat.

"I'm hungry," Ben said. "That emergency ration stuff on the sub was terrible and they never thought to stock the jet."

"We haven't got time to stop for food now," Tom said. Their electro-taxi jerked and swayed as the driver stopped for a boy leading a camel, then for a group of gawking tourists. The cab swerved around a line of veiled women in black, past a liquid plastics truck, and finally hurtled onto the four-lane highway leading toward their destination, Sahara Base.

Aristotle was standing on the rear bumper of the taxi and swiveled his head to look at an electro-car that had pulled out from behind a mud hut. The squat robot ignored the bugs impacting on his body as he watched the car follow them.

"Tom," he said in a voice loud enough to penetrate the cab, "we are being tailed."

"Uh-oh." Tom scrunched around in the seat to look out past Aristotle's metal legs. "Are you certain?"

"Yes. When we slowed for that stray donkey, they had an opportunity to pass and did not. Instead, they have maintained an even distance. I have not been able to identify the occupants as they are wearing cloths across the lower portions of their faces."

"They must be Luna's men," Ben said. "We could let Aristotle off and he could punch a hole in their engine as they go past. That wouldn't violate his programing not to harm humans—they'd just roll to a stop."

"But then they'd probably get out and wreck Aristotle, who would not protect himself," Anita protested.

Tom agreed. "We can't do that," he said. "Besides, we'll need Aristotle later on. He may be only a machine, but . . ." His voice trailed off.

"Yeah, I'm fond of him, too," Ben said. "He kind of grows on you."

"So what do we do?" Anita asked. "It's thirty miles to the spaceport."

Tom thought furiously. They would probably manage to keep ahead of their enemies until there was a straight stretch of highway with no traffic. Then the chase car would catch up and . . . do what?

All around them was nothing but sand, rock, heat, and desolation.

"There's no use having Aristotle radio for help," Tom said, thinking aloud. "Whatever they're going to do, they'll do in the next few minutes. We can't stop, we can't turn, and I won't sacrifice Aristotle."

"Not even for the stardrive?" Anita asked softly.

Tom shook his head firmly. "No. For one thing, Aristotle is the only one to have had extensive communication with Aracta. If anything happens to Aracta, Aristotle is our only hope."

The taxi drove over a slight incline and they could see a straight road ahead. In the distance were shining dots—the buildings on Sahara Base. As they watched, a ship rose on a fountain of brilliant flame, heading upward in space.

Suddenly, Anita's face contorted in pain. Ben saw it and touched her hand in sympathy. She smiled weakly.

Ever since an accident in which the circuits of Anita's artificial right leg were violently combined with the powerful circuits of Aristotle, a condition had existed which was both beneficial and frightening to her. Her powers of empathy had been tremendously escalated. The circuits of her artificial limb, and the complex computer which occupied the space where her calf would have been, were attached directly to her nervous system. This gave her feedback, enabling her to "feel" the floor and to use her artificial foot quite naturally. But the new circuitry had created a heightened awareness in her brain so that she could often sense what someone else was feeling—pain, anger, joy, or sadness.

The intense emotions Tom was experiencing as he sought a solution to their problem had registered heavily on her.

"Tom, they are gaining on us," Aristotle informed the young man.

The driver was now aware that something odd was going on. A look in the mirror made him press the accelerator to the floor. But the electro-car behind them was too powerful and drew closer.

Aristotle sounded urgent. "The passenger has a weapon. It is an automatic rifle in the nine millimeter category. Do you have any instructions?"

Tom gritted his teeth. The robot's calm assessment of the situation showed an inhuman lack of fear. But then, Aristotle was not human, despite their feelings toward him.

"They're pulling out to pass," Ben shouted. "Driver, step on it!"

The old vehicle was doing its best, but that simply wasn't good enough. Tom could see the passenger's arm come out of the window, the rifle in his hand aiming low.

The tires!

They undoubtedly planned to blow out the tires and anyone who survived the wreck would meet with a further "accident." Tom looked around frantically. There was no place to hide, no weapons, no way to evade the killers!

# Chapter Seven

"Look out!" Anita screamed. The electro-cab gave a lurch and swerved, the driver shouting in the Berber language. Tom glanced back and saw that Aristotle had leaped from the rear bumper of the taxi directly into the path of the pursuing car. There was a screech of brakes, a metallic *scrunch,* and the killers' car careened into the desert.

Aristotle was knocked down, but even before Tom could order their driver to halt, the robot was back on his feet, trotting out into the sandy roadside toward the wreck.



Their enemy's vehicle had struck a small boulder and stopped. The two men who occupied it were unconscious. Aristotle started to pull them out before Tom and the others arrived.

"Warning," the robot said. "My sensors detect a malfunction in the power system. The battery has shorted and this car is about to explode."

Tom seized the collar of one of the masked men and dragged him through the sand toward the road. There was a short whine, then a buzzing sound as the rear end of the electro-car exploded.

When all the parts had thumped to Earth, Tom rolled off the man he had shielded from the flying shrapnel. "He's knocked out, but I don't think he's badly hurt," he said as he examined the stranger.

"Same here," said Ben, who had pulled the other man to safety.

Tom turned to Aristotle. "Now, why did you do that?"

"It was the logical option, Tom. You had no weapons, there was no other way to stop them from harming you. I calculated the angle successfully and placed myself in a position to alter the direction of their vehicle."

"You could have been killed!" Anita cried, coming up to examine the robot's outer shell.

"I do not believe *kill* is the proper term to use for an electronic entity," Aristotle corrected her.

"Don't get so particular!" Anita grumbled. "Look at this dent!"

Tom put his fists on his hips. "Listen, you bucket of bolts, you violated basic programing!"

"Oh, no, Tom, I disagree. I dislike being in conflict with you, but I carefully reviewed my options in the matter. While I did not anticipate the boulder they struck, I calculated that they would go off and be stuck in the sand, thus rendered harmless."

Tom smiled. "You're right, Aristotle. Thanks. You saved our lives."

Ben patted the mechanoid on the shoulder, then turned to the two men. "What'll we do with them?" he asked.

"There is a large transportation vehicle approaching now," the robot replied. "I believe the correct term is *bus.* We could turn these men over to the driver and proceed to Sahara Base at top speed."

"He's right," Ben said, getting up and brushing off his clothes. "We don't have time to take them to the hospital, much less to the cops."

"Okay," Tom said, eyeing the bus now coming over the rise. He stepped out into the road and flagged it down.

Sahara Base was a vast, blotched field. Parts of it were concrete, seared and blackened by the many takeoffs. Other sections were concave dishes of dark glass where the roaring fires of rocket exhausts had melted the sand, fusing it into the rough glass.

Along the western edge of the area stood a line of buildings fifty stories high—the assembly structures for the giant rockets that took passengers and cargo up into orbit. Along the eastern edge were passenger terminals, offices of spaceline companies, storehouses, small factories serving the great complex, and residential housing for thousands of people who worked at the field.

Above the tallest of the terminals towered the symbol of the Luna Corporation—a great glittering neon quartermoon. It was eerily reflected nearby in the green and white flag of Algeria.

"Now what?" Ben asked.

"Driver, pull up by those phones," ordered Tom.

They stopped at the edge of the parking lot,

which was mostly filled with tourist buses, and Tom jumped out to call Launch Control. He came back to the taxi with a sad face.

"Missed him!" he exclaimed, pounding his fist on the taxi roof. "A Luna ship, the *Corsair Queen,* took off fifteen minutes ago."

Anita winced slightly. She was having a hard time absorbing all the strong emotion coming from Tom.

"Aristotle," Tom asked, "do we have a ship?"

"Yes, sir. A Mister Jensen, of Swift Enterprises, leased a Jupiter Nine for us."

Ben whistled. "Really?"

"Yes. There was a transmission from Mister Jensen that seems to have become somewhat garbled. Something about it better be worth it."

Tom laughed for the first time in the long, tense day. "Where is the ship?"

"They are preparing it on Launch Pad 78 of the Zeitraum Fluggesellschaft."

"The German space company?" Ben asked. "Hey, those guys really know what they're doing! Let's go!"

They got out of the taxi near a cluster of electro-carts that were available for transporting people around the vast field.

A group of burly-looking men lounged in the shade of some packing crates. They watched Tom and his friends, but most of their attention was on the robot. Their manner did not seem hostile, but it was not particularly friendly, either.

Tom went into the main office and soon emerged with a tall, blond official who addressed one of the men clad in a flight jumper. "Wang! Take these people to J-Nine." He gave Aristotle a speculative look, then pointed to another fellow. "Licudi, you take the robot."

The two men climbed down from the packing crates and hopped into electro-carts. Ben, Anita, and Tom got into the first one.

Their driver, who was Oriental, grinned at Tom. "Name's Chih Hsing Wang. You mudballers must be high-honcho to get a private trip."

"Mudballers?" Tom repeated.

"Sure." The driver started the engine and drove around the building. "The world has two kinds of people—spacers and mudballers." He shot a quick look at Tom. "On second thought, maybe you guys are spacers, after all."

Tom grinned. "Maybe," he said. He looked over his shoulder. Aristotle rode by himself, sitting up with great metallic dignity as the electrocart hummed across the vast field.

The spaceport was huge almost beyond imagination. There were strips of barren desert between great square pods of blast-proof concrete, but the effect was that of a flat cement world.

It was hot. The light gray of the concrete reflected the sun. Tom was grateful for the brief shade as they passed below a gantry and spaceship. Then they drove under the blackened jets of a rocket sitting like a skyscraper on its fins.

Wang sensed the discomfort of his passengers as they eyed the funnel-shaped jets above their heads. "Shortcut," he explained, obviously enjoying himself.

The little two-car parade rolled around the end of a long peninsula of repair sheds, then headed out across a smooth desert. The field was so large that some of the more distant ships seemed sunken in the earth, partially hidden by the curvature of the ground.

Without warning a spattering of concrete sprayed Tom's car on the driver's side. A groove had been blasted in the mottled concrete just beneath them. Wang looked surprised, but Tom knew at once what was happening.

"They're firing at us!" he yelled. A second invisible beam sliced through the awning which gave slight protection from the fierce North African sun and the fabric collapsed into the face of the driver. The car lurched and weaved as Wang fought to regain his sight. It was the erratic course the electro-cart took that saved them.

Spatters of ruptured concrete struck Ben, Tom, Anita, and Wang as more laser-beam shots were fired. Tom twisted around and saw Aristotle's cart veering away as the driver frantically sought shelter.

The nearest protection of any sort was the landing gear of a jet plane almost three hundred yards away. Another laser pulse exploded one of the front tires and Wang almost lost control of the suddenly twisting electro-cart. He finally managed to bring it to a shaky halt.

"Everyone get out on this side," Tom yelled as he jumped to the ground.

Under protection of the cart, they ran toward the jet plane. The concrete ended and they galloped down into a shallow depression between concrete pads. If it rained—which it almost never did—it would have been a flood control channel.

The gully offered little protection, but they threw themselves flat on their stomachs, hoping their attackers would not come any closer.

"Tom, what's happening?" Anita asked, her breath blowing up dust as she pressed herself into the hard-packed sand. "Who's shooting at us?"

"Who else?" Ben muttered. He raised his head slightly and looked toward the point where the firing had originated. He was flat on his face again before Anita could tell him to be careful.

"I saw two men by the repair shed," Ben said. Tom dug into his pocket and pulled out a radio only a couple of inches long.

"Aristotle, come in," he said.

"Yes, Tom?"

"Did you radio for the spaceport police?"

"Yes. I sent a distress signal just as soon as I perceived danger. I have already requested an ambulance."

"Who's hurt?" Tom asked, concerned.

"Mister Licudi has severe cuts and a possible broken forearm. We left the electro-cart in a precipitous manner."

"Are you all right, Aristotle?" Tom asked anxiously.

"Yes. Some slight abrasions to my extremities, but nothing a little bit of polishing will not repair."

Ben popped up for another look and instantly

crouched again, his eyes big. "Tom! They're coming after us! Two guys! With lasers!"

"Luna is taking no chances," Tom muttered, frantically looking around trying to find some kind of escape. Just then a close laser-beam shot turned a strip of sand into a glassy groove.

A second blast dug deeper into the sand. Their attackers were getting closer!

# Chapter Eight

Tom was desperate. They had no weapons and no protection. The spaceport police had not arrived yet and the gunmen would reach them in a few seconds!

Suddenly they heard a yell. Both Tom and Ben took a chance, lifting their heads a few inches. What they saw made them gasp!

Aristotle was racing across the concrete plain, pushing the electro-cart ahead of him. The two thugs were firing at the cart, ripping into the molded plastic with their beams. One of the tires exploded, then another, as the men blasted away at the advancing vehicle.

Aristotle kept pushing. The cart scraped against the concrete in a shower of sparks. The electro-cart started to burn as another volley of laser fire blasted into it.

Then one of the attackers stopped firing. He stared at his weapon a moment, then started to run away. The other man shouted, shot two more long pulses of fire into the burning cart before his weapon, too, emptied.

When he began to run, Aristotle let go of the cart and rolled after the two attackers, but Tom called into the radio, "No, Aristotle. No! Leave them to the police."

"I can ensure they are captured, Tom," Aristotle argued, but he came to a halt, gazing after the two men who had disappeared into the shed area. "I can follow and—"

"*No*! You are too valuable. Let them go!" Tom and his friends got to their feet as Aristotle turned to roll toward them.

Wang happily clapped the robot on the shoulder. "Thanks, pal," he said. "You saved our lives!"

A spaceport police helicopter landed and three officers jumped out. After a quick conference with Tom, they ran toward the repair shed as another white chopper came into view.

"They're going to take us over to the ship," Tom explained. "I told the police that Mister Wang would give an accounting. We don't have much time."

"Sure, I'll be glad to. It's been pretty boring around here lately, stuck on the ground like we've been."

Tom took Anita and Ben aside and whispered to them a moment. They all dug into their pockets, then shrugged. Tom returned to Wang, smiling ruefully. "I'm sorry. We were going to give you a tip, but none of us have any money. Just credit cards."

Wang grinned and shook his head. "That's okay. I've got a terrific story to tell the guys."

Anita tugged at Tom's arm and whispered to him. Then Tom turned to Wang and smiled, "You're having trouble getting back into space?"

Wang shrugged. "You know how it is. Work comes and goes. Right now it's gone."

"Call Mister Jensen at Swift Enterprises, Shopton, New Mexico. Tell him I said to call—Tom Swift—ask him if he can find you some kind of work. In space."

Wang's eyes grew big. "Hey, man, that's—aw, you don't have to do anything like that."

"Come on," Ben said, waving them toward the white helicopter. "Let's go, huh?"

"You call," Tom said, pointing at the driver. "I'll contact him myself once we get out of here. We owe you one."

"Aw, I was just driving . . ."

"You hung in there," Tom said, waving.

They left Wang talking to a spaceport inspector. The white chopper rose, banked, and flew toward the slim needle that was their spacecraft.

A Jupiter Nine was the workhorse of the space shuttle service. Sturdy, as safe as any spacecraft made, it had long ago replaced the old throwaway shuttlecraft.

The fifty-story-high ship went up in one piece and came back to Earth the same way, supported by fold-out wings. It had reusable parts, and thus had made spaceflight cost-effective.

With the cheap power coming from the solar-power satellites, Earth was slowly getting rich. Tom thought that, even without the magical stardrive, by the time he would be an old man everyone on Earth would be affluent. Factories in space, inventions, discoveries, and people with brains had combined to raise the standard of living for the whole world.

A farmer in India learned about agriculture from a village television station receiving programs made in Japan and Australia by way of a satellite manufactured in America. A fisherman on Lake Popo in western Bolivia used a motorboat crafted in England. An Italian racing driver in the Buenos Aires Grand Prix used perfectly spherical ball bearings made in the null-gravity of the *New America* space colony.

An official was standing by their Jupiter Nine, the *Mime,* which Swift Enterprises had arranged for Tom and his friends.

"May I see your licenses and rating cards, please?" he asked crisply, with a slight German accent. After thoroughly inspecting them, he turned to Tom. "Mister Jensen informed me you would be the pilot. Is that correct?"

"Yes. Ben Walking Eagle will be the copilot," Tom replied.

"Then everything appears to be in order," the man said as he stepped aside and allowed them to board the spaceship.

Everyone quickly assumed their positions inside the *Mime* and prepared to take off.

"Launch Control, this is ZFG Flight Fourteen," Ben said into the copilot's microphone.

"ZFG Fourteen, this is Launch Control; you are cleared for immediate launch."

"Roger, Launch Control. ZFG Fourteen out."

"Where is Foster by now, Aristotle?" Tom asked grimly.

"The *Corsair Queen* is maneuvering to dock with *New America* in approximately one hour and eight minutes."

"We'll never catch up," Ben said with great pessimism.

"Aristotle, any reply yet from the director at *New America*?" Tom asked.

"No, I am in constant communication, keeping an open line, but no one wants to take the responsibility and the director is not to be disturbed, they say."

"Do you think the new director, the one that replaced Grotz, is on the payroll of Luna?" Anita asked.

Tom shrugged as he punched out the final launch sequence into the *Mime*'s computer. "David Luna is a very powerful man. People will do things—or not do things—just to stay on his good side without anything so gross as bribery. We—"

A klaxon blared and the entire ship began to

rumble. An invisible pressure shoved them all deep into the thick seatpads. Anita groaned uncomfortably and Ben grunted.

"We're off," he said unnecessarily.

Midway to *New America,* Aristotle turned to Tom. "I am afraid there are new complications," he said.

"What?" asked Tom.

"The director of *New America* has temporarily closed the port to all ships leaving the space colony."

"That's no complication, that's *good* news," Ben exclaimed. "Hurrah! Foster won't be allowed to leave and we'll grab him and Aracta there!"

"No, Ben," Aristotle continued. "The order was given ten minutes after the launching of the Luna Corporation's ship—the *Giannini*—David Luna's personal ship."

"He must be hitching a ride with Luna himself!" Tom suggested.

"Obviously the new director is on Luna's payroll," Anita said angrily. "How will we ever catch Foster now?"

Tom shook his head. "We're not giving up so easily," he said. "There's too much at stake."

He turned back to the ship's controls. "Aristotle, can you find out where the *Giannini* is headed?"

The robot was silent for a few minutes, then replied, "Its destination would appear to be some place in the asteriod belt."

Anita sighed. "Tom, I don't want to be a glum goose, but we have to be realistic about this. Once Foster gets Aracta that far, we've lost. I'm sorry, but out there in space there's a legal question of getting the probe back. It will be decades before the World Court decides who has jurisdiction there, who controls the police and enforces what laws. Meanwhile, the powerful people prevail. Luna could make us disappear and just act innocent. Who's to stop him?"

"We have to be careful," Tom said. "Of course, if you and Ben don't want to go to the asteroids, I'll be happy to swing by *Sunflower,* drop you off, and pick you up on the return trip. I wouldn't blame you for not wanting to go."

Tom was referring to a second space colony which was almost completed.

"Are you kidding?" Ben exploded. "Miss *this*? No way!"

"Oh, Tom," Anita said. Then she saw his mischievous grin. "You knew we'd go along!"

"I suspected you would, but I didn't want to drag you."

"I do not have volition in such matters," Aristotle said from his seat behind them. "But I would like to volunteer, nevertheless."

Tom chuckled. "The Four Musketeers!" he said.

"Well, Three Musketeers and an Electroteer, anyway," Ben said.

"Now we just have to make sure this ship has enough fuel and provisions," Tom said.

"And that the leasing company will extend the contract," Anita put in.

"Will a Jupiter Nine make a trip of this length okay?" Ben asked anxiously.

"Sure," the young inventor said. "They are usually used for shorter distances, but these old workhorses were built for heavy duty."

"Why not try to get another ship at *Sunflower* or on one of the bases on the Moon?" Anita asked.

"Alas," Aristotle put in, "there is nothing available for leasing at *Sunflower* and the only ship available for hire on any of the bases on the Moon is another Jupiter Nine. And that one is considerably older than the *Mime.*"

The next twenty minutes were spent examining supplies and equipment.

"Everything checks out more than adequately," Ben said.

"Good. Now to clear it with Zeitraum Fluggesellschaft," said Tom as he radioed Sahara Base.

The company quickly agreed to lease the *Mime* for a trip to the asteroid belt rather than to *New America.* Swift Enterprises' top credit rating took care of any hesitation the company might have had.

"We're on our way!" Tom exclaimed. "Ben, you and Aristotle plot our new course. We've managed to outwit David Luna this time. I wonder what obstacles he'll come up with next?"

Though he did not say so aloud, Tom suspected the unscrupulous Luna would soon begin to show his true colors again. In all probability, the young inventor and his friends were heading into danger—and heading into it fast!

# Chapter Nine

A few hours later Aristotle came over to the pilot's couch. "It is now possible to say with certainty that Lieutenant Foster is headed for Ceres."

"That makes sense," replied Tom. "Ceres is the largest asteroid and the Luna Corporation has its main base there. For good reason, of course."

"My knowledge of the asteroid belt is limited," Ben said. "Tell me about it."

"Well, strictly speaking, the asteroid belt isn't a belt," Tom explained. "A zone, maybe. Instead of being all nicely packed into one circular or elliptical orbit around the Sun, the asteroid belt is really a ragtag collection of debris left over from the formation of the solar system. It also includes some captured asteroids that happened by, along with, perhaps—and this is a big perhaps—the remains of a planet that didn't quite form when the rest were forming or that broke apart for some reason."

"The shattered planet theory is more romantic," Anita said.

"But why Ceres?" Ben asked. "I know it's the largest asteroid—four hundred and thirty-seven miles in diameter—but why there, exactly?"

"Ceres has a nearly circular orbit and is roughly in the center of the belt, so that it makes the best place from which to centralize operations. Some of these minor planets—or asteroids, if you prefer—wander around quite a bit. Amor, for example. It comes close to Earth's orbit, then goes out beyond Mars, and halfway to Jupiter. Adonis can move so near to the Sun it is almost in the orbit of Mercury, yet its elliptical orbit takes it halfway to Jupiter, too."

"Apollo swings in between Earth and Venus, doesn't it?" Anita asked. "Then well out beyond Mars?"

"Right," replied Tom. "But it is Hidalgo that

has the largest orbit. It doesn't get in any closer than beyond Mars, but it swings way out, well beyond Jupiter, almost to Saturn. There's Hungaria, Thule, Hermes—that one comes within 400,000 miles of Earth—Icarus, Davida, Hebe, Iris, and lots of others."

"Plus a lot of rock, dust, and stuff," Anita said. "They aren't even round—the smaller ones, anyway. Eros looks like a giant peanut!"

Ben grinned. "I feel so dumb. I thought it was just a bunch of big rocks in a circle out beyond Mars."

"There are at least 460,000 asteroids logged so far," Tom said. "That's just the ones somebody figures might be worth visiting someday. Yet, even with a half million rocks out there, the orbit is so large that you probably couldn't see very many from any one asteroid."

"But the Luna Corporation has been getting the cream of the metallic asteroids, hasn't it?" Ben asked.

Tom shrugged. "They aren't the only mining outfit working out there, just the biggest. But even they will have a hard time checking out their thousands of claims." Tom shook his head. "No, it's a colossal project, but incredibly valuable to Earth. From all indications, there is several times more metal in the asteroids than we have mined since the very beginning of history."

Ben whistled in astonishment. "No wonder David Luna has a reputation for playing rough. There's a lot at stake out there!"

Tom agreed. "He's a formidable foe. Right now there's not much we can do but monitor Luna's ship and keep following it. We should get as much rest as we can and then try to prepare for what might happen when we land on Ceres."

He looked at the robot. "Do you have any suggestions or prophecies, Aristotle?"

"No, Tom. Certainly no prophecies. Human behavior is, I am afraid, still something of a mystery to me. A human will have the identical response to a stimulus ninety-nine times and on the hundredth have a totally different one. Yet, in some areas a human being can also be monotonously predictable."

Tom shook his head at the long answer and said to Ben, "Do you think Aristotle is becoming garrulous?"

"He is getting talky, that's for sure!" the computer tech replied.

"I think he's darling," Anita insisted. "What

do you mean about humans being monotonously predictable, Aristotle?"

"It was upon an analysis of behavior of the mercenary assassins that—"

"You mean the thugs that attacked us at the spaceport?" Ben interrupted.

"Precisely, Ben. Based upon numerous cases in my reading, I predicted there was a reasonable possibility that, once deprived of the capabilities of their laser weapons, they would lose their aggressiveness and retreat. That was, in fact, what happened."

"You risked your life on *that?*" Anita said, shocked.

The robot looked at her, his lenses glittering in the cabin light. "I am not alive in the biological sense, Anita. I have great trouble comprehending that humans have faulty memory circuits. You no doubt had that information at one time."

Anita blushed. "Oh, of course, Aristotle, but . . . uh . . . well, I think we all think of you as, well, *alive.*"

"Thank you. I perceive that as a compliment. Human beings have frequent need for complimentary appraisals of their work or actions, I have noticed. This has something to do with their egos, I believe. The ego is another area in which my comprehension is less than perfect."

"If it is any help," Ben commented dryly, "it is for humans, too."

"I did mean that as a compliment, Aristotle," Anita put in hastily.

"And I thank you, Anita. As a flawed mechanism, I find it is indeed warming to my circuits to be considered of value."

Tom laughed and said, "Aristotle, take over the pilot's couch for a while."

"Yes, Tom."

"Let's get something to eat," Tom suggested. "I'll cook."

"Eggs Benedict," Ben said quickly. Seeing Anita's look, he added, "Greatest sauce you ever tasted—if it's done properly."

"They have such a thing on this ship?" Anita asked.

Ben nodded. "You wouldn't believe it. Frozen everything. Natural foods, not processed mud. Remember, this is a commercial ship, not one of those cramped scientific-expedition ones we're used to traveling in. Space is not at a premium here. There's a whole refrigerator full of cheeses. Just cheese!"

The Eggs Benedict turned out to be superb,

and afterward the group sat back in the well-padded living quarters, content to let Aristotle handle the flying.

"What are the bad guys doing right now?" Tom asked. "Has Foster managed to get the secret out of Aracta? Or have the two crazies cancelled each other out?"

Ben yawned. "I think it's time to go to bed. There's nothing we can do about the bad guys tonight and I, for one, am tired."

"Good idea," Anita joined in. "We're going to have to be at our best—and very soon!"

Ceres was a rough sphere ahead. Its rugged surface was pitted with craters.

The Luna Corporation base was in a cluster of domes. While most of the actual base was underground—just as on the Moon—there were repair and storage facilities on the surface. A number of circles had been cleared off and made smooth, dotted with control lights for visual approaches and radar repeaters for automatic landings.

"Will they let us go in?" Anita asked.

Tom made a face. "I don't know. They must know we are here, even if they weren't informed by Sahara Base or *New America.* If I read the great

David Luna correctly, he's pretty sure he can handle us."

"Do you think he is here?" Ben asked.

"I imagine he either was already here or he came out on the *Giannini.* The probe business is too important to leave to underlings."

"Tom, Ceres Control requests identification," Aristotle said.

"We can't say we're just another happy-go-lucky tourist party," Anita said, gesturing around at their ship. "And we surely can't say we're here to recover Aracta—that's calling them thieves."

"Or kidnappers, considering Aracta's self-awareness and intelligence," Ben added.

They all looked at Tom, who sighed mightily. "The truth is, all the way out here I've been trying to think what to do when we got here, and I'm no nearer now than I was when we left. We are simply sailing into the lion's mouth."

"Oh, no. Wait a minute," Ben insisted. "I've seen those movies where the brave hero lets himself be captured and then turns the tables on the bad guys. But not before his chief enemy has first explained how everything works, thus giving our hero the last bit of information he needs to make his getaway, blowing everything up as he goes."

Ben waved his hands in the air. "But that isn't the way it works in real life. In *real* life the bad guy gets the good guy in his clutches and zaps him right away; no long cozy talk over brandy, no boastful explanations—he just kills him, whammo. The end. And this does *not* appeal to me. We'd better think of another way."

"The Indian way?" Tom asked.

"What's that?" Anita asked. "Attack at dawn? Ride around the wagons? Drop from the trees?"

She eyed Ben ironically. "You got any ideas?"

Aristotle spoke again. "Tom, they have requested identification and accompanied it with an option you will not like."

A chill went through everyone in the cabin.

Tom looked at Aristotle tensely. "What's that option?" he asked.

"They will fire on us as a pirate vessel!"

# Chapter Ten

"They can't do that!" Ben growled.

"I'm afraid they can," Tom countered. "There was a theft of iridium ingots several months ago and the Luna Corporation received temporary powers of sovereignty for the near-space area of Ceres." He paused. "All they have to do is declare that we constitute a danger to them."

He turned to Aristotle. "Transmit our ship numbers and ownership. Say we are on a private voyage of discovery and investigation."

"Yes, Tom."

"They'll know that's a lie," Anita stated.

Tom shook his head. "But it isn't. It's just not

the whole story. We are on a voyage of discovery and investigation and it does make us legitimate. They might zap us, but it won't be because they don't know who we are. Aristotle, send a duplicate transmission to Earth."

"Yes, Tom."

"Yeah, but now what?" Ben asked.

"Is the *Giannini* down there?" Tom asked the robot.

"Yes. It has just recently landed. The sensors show considerable heat still in the landing area. In addition, there is a crew servicing the vessel."

"We're too late," Ben muttered. "They had all the way out here to get the information from Aracta. We've lost. Even if we do get the probe back, they'll still have the stardrive, and they've probably started to work on it already!"

"Maybe not," Tom said. "Look, Aracta must have made some kind of deal. Before he gave them any information he must have been reasonably certain that they would fulfill their part of the bargain. And what would that deal be?"

"To help the Skree," Anita said. "Build a fleet of warships, I imagine."

"Has that happened?" Tom asked, gesturing at the screens. "Have they had time? Not if they were converting present ships. They can't get

Earth's space navy. Not even David Luna has that kind of power."

"So what do you think he'll do?" Ben asked.

"He'll attempt to trick Aracta. Get the stardrive and to blazes with helping the Skree. Wars are not profitable any more. Luna is greedy, perhaps greedier than any man in history. He doesn't want to conquer a race or invade and annex a country. He wants a whole star system!"

"Tom, how do you know Luna?" Anita asked.

"Two years ago he approached me," the young man told her. "He's quite charming when he wants to be. We met casually—or so I thought at the time—at a benefit. He donated a staggering sum. He introduced me to a famous author, a couple of beautiful actresses, a senator, and several other people of importance. I was rather flattered, I must admit. Afterward he insisted I come along to his place for dinner."

Tom grinned ruefully and spread his hands. "His place turned out to be a luxury residence attached to the Poseidon dome in the sea off the Azores. Private jets for a huge party, gifts of golden doubloons from a Spanish galleon lost in 1602—"

Anita gasped and Tom nodded. "It didn't seem all that significant at the time, but you can see Luna had a little business on the side. It was all very fancy. A Parisian chef, Maine lobsters, flowers flown in from Hawaii, the works."

Tom sighed, then continued. "He got me alone and said that with my brains and his power we could rule the world. Oh, he didn't use those words, but that was what he meant. He wanted me to leave my father's company. The words he used were 'trying out your own wings.' When I refused, he laid it on thickly. He gave me hints of what he had in mind—a monopoly on asteroid mining—but not how he planned to get it: certain tax advantages, political power, holding companies. He even suggested how one might use solar-power collectors as immense rayguns to cripple an enemy on Earth."

"How horrible!" Anita said.

"I think it's funny," Ben said lightly. "Did you sell your soul, Tom? Did you get eternal youth, riches, and a credit card that never sends bills?"

"It's not funny, Ben," Anita said. "That man was serious."

"He *was* serious," Tom said. "When he at last understood I was not about to join him, he became, just for a moment, the man I expected him to be. It definitely was not a pretty sight. He's a vindictive man and he scares me. Anyone who isn't scared of someone like that is . . . well, not paying attention."

"They are waiting for us to land," Ben said. "They'll arrange an accident down there—something terminal."

Aristotle spoke up. "Tom, an incoming message."

"Put it on the speaker."

"—ing *Mime.* Come in. This is Ceres Control calling *Mime.* Come in, please."

Tom thumbed the microphone, keeping off the visual channel. "Ceres Control, this is the *Mime*. Over."

"*Mime.* Please hold for Mister Luna."

Tom's eyebrows went up and he looked at his companions. "The boss, himself!"

"Ah, Mister Swift, I believe? The younger Mister Swift? How are you, dear boy? Are you coming to see us?" Luna laughed quite heartily. "Of course, you are. The other mining claims are almost on the other side. Do land, Mister Swift. I am preparing a banquet which I'm sure will delight you."

"Hemlock and toadstools, I'll bet," Ben muttered from the side of his mouth.

"Will the guest list include Lieutenant Foster?" Tom asked.

"Of course! He has just arrived, as I'm certain you know. We had a most engaging conversation regarding his employment with us."

"No retirement benefits, I imagine," Ben grumbled.

"You *are* aware that Foster stole the alien memory core from Swift Enterprises and that you are harboring a fugitive?"

"No, Mister Swift. As I understand it, the entity in the memory core—and we recognize his self-awareness and personal sovereignty, naturally—is a free agent able to make his own decisions. No, theft is certainly not the proper term here. Escort, perhaps? Accompaniment?" The billionaire laughed again.

"I'm certain all those brilliant lawyers to whom I pay such extravagant retainers would be only too eager to earn their money for me," Luna continued. "It is certainly not a matter of ownership, dear me, no. You can't own anyone, at least, not anymore. No, indeed, my dear fellow. While Mister Aracta is not legally a citizen of any nation in this system, I think you will recognize this as a precedent. He *is* a free entity and entitled to all courtesy and assistance as a representative of an intelligent race."

"You're right, Tom," Anita murmured. "He is smooth."

"And he just may be digging his own grave." Tom turned to his robot. "Aristotle, is this being microwaved back to earth?"

"Yes. To Swift Enterprises' Central Communication."

Tom switched on the mike once again. "We accept your invitation—all three of us." Aristotle turned his head around to look at Tom, but the young inventor waved a hand at him. "We'll land as soon as your traffic control permits."

"Tom—" Ben said, warningly.

"You are most gracious," Luna replied. "It is not often we have visitors here. I will return you to your people. Until we meet again, Mister Swift."

Tom spoke with authority. "Aristotle, take over. But make it the slowest landing you can. I need time."

"Yes, Tom."

"Tom, what are you *doing*?" Ben demanded.

"Getting us within reach of Aracta. We can't shoot our way in."

"If half of what they say about this Luna character is true, he's about as safe as a dragon with a toothache!"

Tom left the control room with Ben and Anita trailing behind. "What are you up to?" Anita asked.

"I'm going to the workshop aft. And I'll need you in about half an hour."

The two stopped, puzzled. Ben sighed and slapped his thighs helplessly, then plopped into one of the comfortable chairs. "Well, Prince Valiant went into an enemy's castle disguised as a troubadour once. I wonder if Tom can sing?"

"You're a big help," Anita said. "Who's Prince Valiant?"

"Aleta's husband, Arn's father, and the son of King Aguar."

The redhead eyed him. "You're getting strange, Benjamin Franklin Stumbling Eagle, do you know that?"

The actual landing was routine. Ceres Control fed a series of coordinates into the shipboard computer—which Aristotle immediately rechecked—and they lowered the ship on a plume of fire.

With orders to stay aboard and to prevent any

entry, Aristotle remained in the control room while his spacesuited companions climbed out of the hatch and boarded a small surface vessel that was sent for them. Meanwhile, everything they said was transmitted to the *Mime,* taped, and transmitted to Earth.

The Luna Corporation's dome complex was hardly luxurious. It was a vast processing plant where metal and minerals were smelted out of high-grade asteroids brought into close orbit and broken up with explosives and lasers. The ore was fed into the sun-hot flare of a fusion torch where the material was stripped to its molecular structure, then magnetically transferred along a path—called a mass accelerator—where the various elements dropped out according to weight. Ingots of pure metal and other elements were then put into lightweight metal containers and sent on a long, curving path to Earth's orbit.

Since the trip would take several years, none of the canisters had arrived yet, but there were hundreds on their way, and tests of the accuracy of their approach at predetermined landing sites had been made.

"This place is a gold mine!" Ben said in the decontamination chamber.

"The cores of most planets are metal," Tom

said. "What appears on the surface is only a fraction of any world's metal. The asteroids are, in effect, the metal heart of an entire planet."

"Coupled with cheap solar energy—wow!" Ben exclaimed. "We will all get rich in space! Not just guys like Luna, but everyone!"

The inner hatch cycled open before they could say more. A tall, powerfully built man awaited them. He was dressed in a conservatively cut, dark jumpsuit; he had a brutal, scarred face and a rough voice.

"Mister Swift? I'm Anvil, Jonathan Anvil. Would you and your companions follow me, please? Mister Luna is waiting for you."

Behind his back, Anita nudged Ben and pretended to shiver. Anvil led them through the gray hallways, past storage rooms, pumping plants, and the heat of a fusion torch chamber.

They looked down cross-corridors, although internal airlock hatches kept them from seeing too far. They passed through another dome—a vegetable greenhouse—supplying both food and fresh oxygen. They skirted along the recreational area of a structure where rough miners drank and brawled, then through an airlock marked PRIVATE, and found themselves in a quiet passageway where walls were made of laser-cut slabs of beautiful Cerean rock.

"This way," Anvil said. He opened a set of doors made by a famous metal sculptor and ushered them into a large, comfortable room. "Please make yourselves at home. Mister Luna will be with you in just a moment."

Anvil left and they glanced around. The walls were stocked with tape cassettes of books, films, and music of all kinds. Tom noticed a reel of *To the Land of the Electric Angel,* a much-anticipated film which had not yet been released on Earth.

Ben pointed out an original Schirmeister and two Picassos hanging on the paneled walls. They were looking at a small, prehistoric bronze when the doors opened and David Luna came in.

# Chapter Eleven

The three young people stared at the man in tense silence. He was well-built, medium-sized, and dark-haired. His sharp eyes were penetrating.

"Mister Swift!" he exclaimed. "How good to see you. And Miss Thorwald!" He turned to Ben. "I'm not sure how to address you. Mister Eagle or Mister Walking Eagle?"

"Ben is fine," the Indian boy said uncomfortably.

Luna turned to Tom again. "How is your father these days, may I ask?"

"We've come here to—"

"For dinner!" the industrialist finished for him. He gestured to the opposite set of doors. "This way, please."

The doors were opened by a servant in a dark jumpsuit. Beyond lay a formal dining room. The far wall was a large glassite port looking out upon the Cerean plain and the rim of a crater in the distance.

"Please, Miss Thorwald, sit here next to me," Luna said suavely. "Tom, Ben, sit there." He pointed and laughed softly, indicating the circular table. "This solves so many problems of etiquette, doesn't it? This way everyone sits near the host."

Luna turned to Anita. "Such lovely hair. Charming. Redheads have a very interesting genetic history, are you aware of that? Oh, you're blushing!"

"I am not!" Anita snapped, then looked contrite.

"Yes, it is most difficult to accept compliments, is it not? One usually overdoes it with excessive modesty or else one becomes mock-pretentious, claiming even the most extravagant praise is all but an insult. I assure you, my flametressed beauty, that none of my praise is flattery."

"Mister Luna—" Tom began.

"Not on an empty stomach, Tom, please." To the servant he said, "Would you see what is holding up Lieutenant Foster."

Ben and Tom exchanged looks. Anita still had her eyes downcast, though her color had returned to normal.

"Do you come to the asteroids often, Tom?" Luna asked. "I'm rarely here, of course. Only the most urgent sort of business ever brings me this far into space." He gestured at the formal room with its candelabra and magnificent window. "Very crude, of course, but one must expect to rough it out here on the frontier, mustn't one?" He touched Tom's sleeve. "Of course, if all goes well, the human frontier will be considerably extended."

Again, before Tom could speak, Luna distracted them. "Ah, the soup—really one of the better things here. The Ceres soil, for some reason I can't imagine, grows the most extraordinary vegetables! Simply superb!"

They had just started to eat when the doors opened and Burt Foster appeared. Tom was surprised that the darkly-handsome young man was no longer wearing the uniform of the United States Navy with its distinctive space service insignia, and then Tom realized that he shouldn't be surprised. It was obvious that Foster was going after bigger stakes than a military career.

The former lieutenant walked in with an arrogance that was almost a swagger. He sneered at the visitors and Tom noticed the briefest shadow of annoyance flicker across Luna's face.

"Well, the losers," Foster said. He sauntered to his place at the table, looking at Ben, whose barely suppressed fury was becoming evident, and laughed.

Ben reacted as if slapped in the face. He jumped to his feet. "Traitor!" he snapped. "Turncoat. *Thief!*"

"Please, please, no rancor, my friends!" Luna exclaimed. "Foster, do sit down." When the ex-officer made no move, Luna's voice grew hard. "Sit down. Mister Foster . . . please." The last word was delivered in a silky tone and Foster sullenly obeyed. A servant appeared, placing a bowl of soup in front of him almost at once. Foster stirred it carelessly, but did not eat.

"I apologize to you," Luna said to his other

guests, "but you must understand Mister Foster's state of mind. He was wrongly accused by a biased court—"

Ben snorted and Anita made a strangled sound.

"—and all chances of a significant naval career dissipated, so . . . " Luna prolonged the word, " . . . he chose to assist in the escape of an alien entity from unjust imprisonment." Luna spread his hands in a practiced gesture of inevitability.

"So you claim that what he did was legal?" Tom asked in a calm voice.

"Indeed," replied Luna. "What else?"

"Such information as the alien probe—I mean Aracta—has is for all of mankind!" Anita said.

"Oh?" Luna queried, and Foster glowered at her. "And what, then, was the public-spirited Swift Enterprises doing, tucking Aracta away in a secret laboratory? Weren't you seeking this information for your own advantage?" He held up his hand as all three of his guests started to reply. "Oh, please—I don't blame you one bit. That's just what I would have done. In fact, it is exactly what I *am* doing. Enlightened self-interest is a marvelous motivating force."

"The devil quotes scripture," muttered Anita.

"Please, my dear, I am a businessman. Tom's

father is a businessman. *Tom* is a businessman, as much as he would like to think otherwise. He invents things, patents them, and reaps enormous profits from the fruits of his endeavors." Luna beamed at Tom. "I'm sure you understand, dear boy. Information is power. It's an advantage. It's . . . business."

"Monkey business," Ben said grumpily.

Luna laughed with apparent happiness. "My dear young man—business is business. The law of supply and demand. You sell and buy from people you dislike as well as those you like. You become partners with people you would not care to have dine in your home."

At this, Foster glared at Luna, but the industrialist merely smiled. "Mister Foster here had a supply of something quite unique, and for which there is a great demand. Yes, a *great* demand."

"That stardrive is for whoever can help the Skree against their aggressors," Tom said.

"Of course," David Luna agreed. "We're working on that."

"Then you have the stardrive?" Tom asked cautiously.

"No, but it is merely a matter of time," Luna replied.

Burt Foster looked sternly at Tom. "I can talk

to the thing, Swift. I don't need any fancy robot. I talk to it and it talks to me."

"It?" Ben muttered, looking at Tom.

"You can talk to Aracta because our robot taught him how," Anita said heatedly.

Tom turned to David Luna. "Have you spoken to the probe?"

Luna raised his dark eyebrows. "No, I have no need. The estimable Mister Foster speaks for me."

"So you don't yet have the secret?" Tom persisted.

"Not yet, no, Mister Swift. But it won't be too long."

"I suppose you have Aracta on some kind of rack, pulling out his version of fingernails or threatening him with—" Anita's angry tirade was interrupted by Luna.

"*Please,* Miss Thorwald! Do you think me a monster? Surely not! Mister Foster, I ask you, are we conducting such a campaign?"

Foster's good looks were marred by his anger. He all but sneered at Anita. "How would you persuade something that has a deadly weapon built into it, a weapon you can't take away or disarm?" he snorted. "You trick it, that's what you do, Miss Uppity! You convince it you are its friend, what else?"

Luna seemed annoyed at Foster's frank confession. "What the zealous Mister Foster means is that you use logic—not force."

Tom smiled. "You make him an offer he can't refuse?"

"Yes, I suppose you could say that," Luna agreed smoothly.

"Let's stop beating around the bush," Foster said heavily. "Junk these null-brains and let's get on with it. I have plans."

Luna stared at him through eyes that suddenly seemed made of chips of slate. "Tom Swift is hardly a null-brain, my dear Mister Foster. I, too, have plans and they pivot on one thing . . . and you know what that is."

Foster gazed at his soup. "Yeah, yeah, but this thing is alien—really alien. It asks questions instead of answering them. It *thinks* differently, blast it!"

"I should hope so," Luna said drily. "If it didn't, we wouldn't have a stardrive. Mister Swift, you are an intelligent young man. You know how limited my options are in this unfortunate affair. I have no desire to harm you or your friends. I want you to believe that fully."

"But—?" Tom said with a half-smile.

"But . . . alas, I have no choice. If you were not who you are, if you were not so prominent, not so well-connected, I might be able to put you in a kind of limbo for a bit. Later on, if you made any complaint, my lawyers would take care of that." He spread his hands again, palms up. "But you see my position, I'm sure."

"What is it to be?" Ben asked bitterly. "A walk out of the airlock? Some kind of accident?"

Luna smiled wearily. "I really hate to do this. However, doing business this way is sometimes unavoidable. I only wish—"

The dining room doors crashed open and the dark, muscular figure of Jonathan Anvil appeared.

"Anvil!" snapped Luna. "What is this?"

"We've detected a pulse signal coming from here, sir! Micropulses at random intervals. We've also traced micropulses being broadcast from Swift's ship back to Earth."

Luna sat back in his chair and his face hardened into a mask. "They were searched electronically, weren't they?"

"Yes, sir, as they passed through the airlock. No weapons, but . . . "

"But what?"

"The woman has a false lower leg. The circuitry was analyzed, but it seemed a standard prosthetic limb."

Luna looked at Tom who shrugged. "Yes, it's true," the young man said and got up slowly and walked around to Anita. "I'll take it out. Anita?"

She lifted her leg and pulled up the elastic bottom of her cuff, freeing it from the boot. Tom popped the casing and reached in, clicking loose a small microchip. He tossed it across the table toward Anvil. "Check it out. It sent everything said here back to the ship, compressed into micro-second impulses, and from the ship to Earth."

"You've lost, Luna!" Ben said happily. "All your plans and boasts—revealed!"

Luna smiled through tight lips. "Not quite, Mister Walking Eagle. *Anvil!*"

The aide, who had been examining the chip closely, dropped it to the floor and crushed it under his heel.

Tom calmly sat down again. "You'll find the signals have ceased now. However, the damage has been done."

"You think wrongly," Luna said, a harsh edge to his voice. "No one will care a fig how I got the stardrive. I will be applauded as a hero of mankind, the man who opened the door to the stars! You, Mister Swift, and the rest of you, will be a footnote in history—the ones who tried to stop me and seize the secret for yourselves."

Anita winced sharply. Her empathic powers could not help picking up Luna's gloating and Foster's vindictiveness. The strong emotions were beginning to make her ill.

"You may be right," Tom said. "History shows that good guys don't always win."

"Let's get this over with," Foster said with undisguised viciousness. "Now!"

# Chapter Twelve

"I'm afraid Mister Foster is right," Luna said. "Anvil, would you be so kind as to deliver these people to detention? I will test the reaction on Earth before I make my final decision regarding their disposal."

Ben rose with a roar and stepped on his chair to launch himself across the table at Luna. He struck the industrialist in the chest, sending both him and the chair flying backward. In the light gravity they tumbled wildly for a moment, but the athletic figure of Jonathan Anvil crossed to the struggling pair with startling speed. One explosive karate blow collapsed Ben, and Luna scrambled to his feet in an undignified manner, his face purple with rage.

"He *struck* me! That *idiot* attacked me!" Luna viciously kicked at the unconscious young man.

Anvil had turned toward Tom and Anita after striking Ben with his gloved fists ready for a fight. But Tom had made no move. He hadn't even risen from his chair.

"Does this mean we won't get dinner?" he asked in a calm voice.

Luna did not answer, but made a rough gesture of dismissal with his hand. Anvil reached down and picked Ben up by the collar. Then he motioned to Tom and Anita, pointing to the door. The two started out and Anvil followed, dragging Ben unceremoniously behind him.

"The soup was excellent," Tom said politely. "My compliments to the chef."

"Move it," Anvil growled.

Ben awoke with a groan and glanced around bleary-eyed. He spotted Tom sitting on a metal bunk. The young inventor casually put his hand to his mouth, his finger signaling silence.

"Feeling better?" he asked.

Ben groaned and touched his neck. "What did

he hit me with, a lead glove?" He arched his back and stretched, but his eyes were on Tom, who had his hand up to his eye.

*Television cameras!*

Tom's other hand spider-walked along his arm and Ben understood.

*Bugged.*

"Where's Anita?" he asked.

"In here," she called, and Ben realized there was another cell next to theirs.

"I wonder if they need a whole cell block in this place?" Ben muttered, massaging his neck. He peered at Tom from under the cover of his arm and his other hand massaged his lower right leg. Tom understood and nodded imperceptibly, confirming that the second transmitter was still intact in Anita's artificial leg. He had only removed the decoy transmitter—the other being disguised as part of her biofeedback system. That meant Aristotle would still get microsecond pulses at random intervals, but with a ninety-minute delay after the first transmitter stopped sending.

"How long was I out?" Ben asked.

"About an hour, maybe longer. They took our watches, so I'm not sure."

The first new pulse would go out soon, Ben

thought. Would Luna's people monitor it? What would happen if they caught it?

"How's Aristotle?" he asked, stretching out wearily on the thin cot.

"I suppose he's okay," Tom said. "He has orders not to let anyone in and I think Luna would hesitate to destroy the entire ship. The damage—such as it was—has been done. There's nothing more Aristotle can send."

Ben knew that the last part was for the benefit of the hidden ears. "What do you think Luna will do to us?" he asked.

"Arrange an accident," Anita said loudly. "Send us off in the *Mime* with a bomb aboard or put one of the half-million rocks into a collision orbit or—"

"All right, Anita," Tom said. "But he might have let us go if you hadn't hit him!" The last was a viciously-delivered accusation to Ben, who blinked.

"I just—" Then Ben caught on. Perhaps Tom wanted Luna to think there was dissension in their ranks. He assumed an angry attitude. "Hey, wait a minute, Swift!" Ben sat up, then groaned as his head seemed to come off in chunks. "Are you blaming me for trying to escape?"

Ben saw Tom put his thumb and forefinger together quickly in the ancient okay sign as he answered, "It was foolish. I believe in trying diplomacy and reason."

"Well, reason yourself out of this cell, Swift! The only thing a guy like Luna respects is strength—power and strength!" Ben warmed up to the game they were playing for the television cameras.

"He's a businessman, you know that," Tom said casually. "We might have bought or bargained our way free."

"Yeah, with what? Luna's richer than your father."

"You remember what Aracta told us about—" Tom stopped suddenly, as if realizing for the first time that someone might be listening. He leaned forward and whispered into Ben's ear. "This place might be bugged. We can't let Luna know about . . . you understand."

"Right," responded Ben in a low tone. Then, louder, in a voice tinged with fakery, he said, "Aw, you're as crazy as Foster. Aracta's nutty, too. This whole *thing* is completely insane! Nobody's got a weapon like that, not even some out-of-the-way race in the stars!"

Tom made a show of silent anger and walked to the solid metal door, putting his hands behind his back. Ben noticed the okay sign again.

Now what? he thought. Did they have something to bargain with? Would their enemies detect the next set of micropulse transmissions?

"Listen, Tom," Ben muttered. "I'm sorry I hit that guy. It was foolish of me. But he made me mad!"

Tom turned around. "All right, Benjamin. I saw no purpose in it and the results are predictable, but I share your frustration. I only hope Aracta hasn't revealed too much." He went to lie down on the narrow cot, fearful of overplaying his hand by talking too much about the supposed secret that Aracta had given them. The clever lie was bait, something to give them room to negotiate.

The boys sat in silence wondering if their charade would pay off.

Ben was just drifting off into an uncomfortable sleep when the small window in the door to their cell opened with a loud squeak.

"Okay, you two," a guard said through the small opening. "Let's go."

"Where?" asked Tom.

"Boss wants to see you."

"What's he want to see us about?" Ben asked, barely able to keep the glee out of his voice. He looked at Tom and, very slowly, winked. Luna had fallen for their plan!

"Never mind. Just follow me—and no funny stuff!" the guard retorted sharply.

The opening slammed shut and the two boys heard the jangle of a key chain, then the scrape of a key being inserted into the lock.

"Hey, wh—" the guard called. Then there was a thump, as if a body had fallen to the floor.

This was followed by a loud click and the heavy door to their cell swung open.

"Greetings, Tom . . . Ben," said Aristotle.

"Aristotle!" both boys exclaimed.

"How did you get here?" Ben asked.

"All in good time. If you will simply follow me," the robot said.

Stepping casually over the fallen guard, Aristotle selected a key from the ring he had taken from him and freed Anita.

"Boy, are you a sight for sore eyes," the redhead cried as she threw her arms around the squat mechanoid and kissed him.

"How very nice to see you, Anita. But I am not a boy. Your memory circuits are malfunctioning again. I am also very sorry your eyes are not well.

Nevertheless, we must not stand here chatting. Time is extremely precious, so we must not consume any more of it in idle talk."

The three friends followed the robot down the corridor to another massive door. Aristotle pointed something at the metal panel and a blue-white flame shot from it. Tom recognized the weapon as a message laser designed to send signals back to Earth but now modified and converted into a weapon.

Outside were two burly guards lying crumpled on the floor.

"I concocted a sleep gas in the ship while you were at dinner," Aristotle explained. "I anticipated the necessity for a non-lethal weapon."

"Good old Aristotle," Ben praised the robot as they made their way into the outside passages.

"Old?" the robot said in toneless surprise. "Am I considered obsolete so soon? Tom, I was activated less than a year ago—"

"He's kidding, Aristotle, he's kidding. It's a term of affection."

"I register the exception as distinguished from a statement on chronological age."

"You'll never change," Ben said as they neared an intersection.

"I sincerely hope that I do," Aristotle replied.

"Unless you meant that as a direct order to remain static. I fully plan to expand my awareness of sentient beings as much as permitted by circumstances."

"That's what I mean," Ben said, edging around the corner. They sprinted to another intersection as an alarm noisily went off.

Men tumbled out of rooms ahead of them, saw them, but had no idea what was going on. Tom bullied his way through, saying, "Make way, make way! Priority business for Mister Luna! Make way!"

The bluff worked and they broke free of the crowd, turning down a corridor marked EXIT TO SURFACE. Within a few strides the smooth metal floors of the halls gave way to bare rock. The passage began to incline and they were puffing by the time they made it to the top.

At a curved corridor Tom guessed they were at the foundation of the main dome. But which way should they go?

"Right or left?" he asked Aristotle.

"The main airlock and the *Mime* are to the right direction. But I imagine my entry stirred up considerable response—"

Ben laughed, then groaned as he felt his neck and said, "I imagine it did!"

"What's to the left?" Tom asked, pointing in that direction.

"Ancillary domes, the airlock entrances for the tractors bringing in ore to the fusion torches."

Without comment, Tom began to trot toward the left of the Ceres complex, followed by the others. Aristotle brought up the rear, his eyes facing backward and his auxiliary lenses looking ahead.

They passed through more airlocks, all of which had been automatically closed when the alarm went off. Aristotle's laser sliced through everything. Each cut, however, used up precious time, and Tom was beginning to wonder how much longer it would be before the guards reached them.

A man in a white, stained jumper suddenly appeared, but Aristotle rolled straight at him, the formidable laser pointed at his chest. The man quickly retreated. A few moments later, a group of six fusion workers carrying bars of metal and long wrenches came their way. No one wanted to tangle with a robot carrying a laser.

A long, smoking scar suddenly appeared at head height along the green corridor. Tom saw the lean figure of Jonathan Anvil far behind them aiming a laser weapon at them.

"Yipe!" said Ben, jumping through an airlock hatch that Aristotle had just opened. Another fiery red line went splashing off the edge of the hatch near where Tom's head had been seconds before.

"Close it!" Tom yelled, and they swung the hatch shut. "Better fuse it!" Tom added, and the robot sealed the door with a long welding seam.

"That'll hold him!" Ben exclaimed, but Tom shook his head.

"He knows this place better than we do—he'll find a way around." Tom took off again, running fast, and the others followed.

At an intersection, the young inventor stopped again and turned to his companions. "We can't just make our escape and leave Aracta in the hands of David Luna!"

"Agreed, but where is he?" Anita asked.

"I might be able to answer that," Aristotle said, pointing at a computer terminal down the corridor in front of them. The robot silently wheeled toward it. A man driving an electro-cart piled with metal ingots took one look and abandoned his vehicle to make a run for his life. His cart rolled ahead until it struck a wall.

At the terminal, Tom watched Aristotle's nimble metal fingers fly over the buttons. A map appeared on the screen, replaced almost at once with another, larger-scale map, then several sets of numbers and pages of information.

The squat robot turned to the humans. "I have located a prohibited area—the only one outside the detention cells. That must be where—" The robot stopped in mid-sentence. "I am truly a flawed mechanism." He turned with incredible swiftness and punched out orders to the central computer.

"Aracta is, indeed, in the prohibited area."

"How do you know for sure?" Tom asked.

"I spoke with him."

# Chapter Thirteen

"What?" Tom was flabbergasted.

"I am ashamed of not thinking of it at once," Aristotle replied. "When I was originally conversing with Aracta he requested access to commercial and other channels. I imagined it might be the same case here. While there are no commercial channels, there is a rather large central computer. I asked for the location of any high-speed information requests. Naturally, by this means, I found Aracta. I immediately sent back a message piggy-backed on a routine library request and then Aracta responded by calling me via my contact in the central computer."

"Aw, all you computers stick together!" Ben said, but he was smiling.

"And—?" Tom asked.

"I gave Aracta a copy of all the micropulse transmissions to date and let him make up his own mind. I know he ran a voiceprint check on all of you and on David Luna."

"*And*—?" Tom asked again.

"It is possible he sees that he has been lied to and used in a most shameful way. Aracta is contemplating the lesser of two evils—correction—three evils: David Luna and his exploitive methods which may mean no assistance to the Skree at all; you, Tom, and what you represent as the nobler aspects of the human race; and, lastly, none of the above."

"What do you mean by none of the above?" Anita asked.

"He means Aracta may not give the stardrive to Luna or to us," Tom said thoughtfully.

He turned to Aristotle. "If Aracta had his original exo-skeleton—that is, his ship—would he simply move on in hopes of finding another race?"

"I believe he would consider that possibility. It is a logical option. However, I am unable to determine what the time factor is or just how long

Aracta and the other probes have. I do not believe it is very long, however. Such a factor would weigh heavily in—"

"There they are! Get 'em!" Several burly men were coming at a run with weapons in their hands. Tom and his friends ran around the corner and Tom yelled at Aristotle to follow.

The dented robot was aiming his laser weapon down the passage. Then, with Tom staring and lifting a hand in protest, Aristotle fired. The single laser pulse ripped through an overhead pipe bearing water used to cool the area around the fusion torch. It was so hot it enveloped the entire area in a cloud of steam!

The curtain of steam effectively stopped the advancing men as Aristotle turned to wheel down the corridor calmly. Tom followed, shaking his head at the robot's constant skirting of his programing not to harm human beings.

After a few more moments of traveling along the crooked paths behind tanks through a circuitous route that could only be followed by someone with a perfect map-memory, they came to the edge of the security area.

The walls and floors were painted bright red and the ceilings were lit with bands of soft light.

Guards in red and black uniforms stood at various doors. However, none of them had gas masks and Aristotle simply wheeled into the corridor, squirting knockout gas at the enemies.

Tom followed, thumbing the opening mechanisms on each door to look inside.

In the third room he found Aracta lying on a table with wires going from connections on his surface to various outlets.

"It is about time, my good fellow," Aracta said with an English accent. "I have been kept waiting far too long."

The young people stared in surprise.

"He talks with an English accent," Ben sputtered.

"Mayfair, I believe," Aracta said loftily. "I am denied the additional information that body language gives to one's statements, but I have found that most people are affected by accent, adversely or positively, and I simply selected one that seemed best for my purposes."

"What *are* your purposes?" Tom asked. He hated to take the time, but not knowing how the alien probe would react if he grabbed it, he had no choice but to continue the conversation.

"My purposes are singular, dear fellow. One purpose and one purpose only—to free the race that gave me consciousness! Their survival is my sole concern. It matters not how many races might be exterminated in this endeavor, but the Skree *must* survive!"

The motionless ovoid's voice came from a small hole and sounded very realistic.

"Your language is quite inadequate for me to express how strongly I feel on this subject. Your race—if selected—will be amply rewarded for its sacrifice, as will any other races that assist my masters. Those that survive, that is."

Tom and Ben exchanged a quick look. Aracta was still quite mad, cheerfully obliterating whole races in order to save the Skree.

Aristotle rolled into the room and there was an exchange of rippling squeals that astonished Ben and Tom and made Anita jump. "What was that?" she demanded.

"High-speed transmission," Tom said. He turned to Aristotle. "What have you learned?"

"Aracta confirms my analysis of David Luna's ultimate intentions and he requests that you transport him away from this immediate location."

"What about the stardrive?" Ben asked. "Will we get it or not?"

"Please, Ben, first things first," Tom said. "If we don't get away it'll all be academic. Aristotle, you take Aracta."

There was another exchange of squeals and Aristotle picked up the egg-like alien probe and detached the wires from the outlets. Then he inserted three of the wires leading from the egg into his own exterior connectors, unplugged any unused wires, and they all walked out.

"Where to?" Anita asked.

"Aristotle, show us the way to some spacesuits, then to the surface," Tom ordered.

"Yes, Tom." The robot stepped over debris that had been left in the corridor and they sped through another maze of service passages and ingot warehouses without encountering any opposition. As they neared one of the surface airlocks, Tom saw a guard detail of six tough-looking men waiting with weapons.

He dodged back before they noticed his group. "Gas 'em," he said to Aristotle.

"I am sorry, Tom. I did not anticipate such an extensive use of the gas. I have only a few centiliters left. Not enough, I am afraid, to do the job."

"Tom," Ben said quickly. "Aristotle can shoot with an accuracy that no human could possibly match. Have him shoot the weapons out of their hands. That won't hurt anyone."

Before Tom could comment, Aristotle said, "Unable to complete such an order. The laser is depleted. It would take at least an hour charging its battery to be capable of six such shots, not to mention a safety margin."

"Oh, great!" Anita sighed, leaning back against the wall. "You mean we're out of ammo of every kind?"

"Not quite," Aracta spoke from its cradle in Aristotle's arm. "If you chaps could be of assistance, I might effect our escape."

"Jolly good," Ben said, then looked sheepish. "What's your plan?"

"As it happens, old boy, I am not completely helpless. I have one or two good tricks up my sleeve, but I am afraid I have to get closer."

Tom blinked and fought back a desire to chuckle. An alien probe with such an accent was just ridiculous. "What do we have to do?"

"If you could somehow conspire to get me within five or six yards, I would be able to overcome the rogues and all will be well."

"Do you need a steady firing platform?" Tom asked the ovoid. "Or is it possible for you to shoot from a moving position?"

"I'm afraid you have misunderstood my weaponry capabilities, dear boy. The action I have in mind will not harm anyone in any permanent way. I do not intend to use anything like your laser."

"Do you *have* a laser?"

"I decline to answer, old sport, top secret and all that. Just get me close enough, Gunga Din, and we'll get the job jolly well done."

"Gunga Din?" Anita raised her eyebrows.

"I read all your English literature," Aracta said. "I responded rather well to stories of the glorious days of the British Empire. Those stories do not approximate recorded history, but I suppose that is why they call it fiction."

"*All* of it?" Anita asked. "You read *everything?*"

"He had over three hours on Channel C with a direct connection to the Library of Congress," Aristotle said.

"Yes, but three hours is only . . . oh . . ." Anita said. "High-speed transmission. Three seconds for all of Kipling, a few nanoseconds for the latest best seller, a minute or two for all the poets . . . I see."

"Hey," Tom said. "Never mind that. I have a plan. Ben, find something to wrap Aracta up in. Anita, fix yourself up as though you'd been in a fight. Mess your hair up, dirty your face." To Aristotle he said, "Are there women here on Ceres?"

"Forty-one, Tom. Their functions are varied, from fusion-torch assistant chief to chef, from tug pilot to hydroponics controller."

"Good! I was hoping Anita wouldn't be the only one."

Ben held up a torn sheet of balloon plastic of the kind used for packing. "All I could find. Will this work?"

"Excellent." Tom looked at Anita, who had ripped the shoulder of her jumpsuit and put a smear of grease from a nearby emergency pump across her cheek. She had also dusted herself with things out of a trash container.

"I look terrible," she said with a rueful smile.

"You look perfect," Tom said. He asked Aracta, who was disconnected from Aristotle and wrapped in the plastic sheet, "Can you be dropped safely?"

"Certainly, old chap," Aracta replied. "I was made to be all but indestructible. Just give me clearance."

"All right," Tom said. "Anita, you stagger out there carrying Aracta. Hold on to one end of the sheet. Act like someone is after you, mumble and yell things like 'Fire!' 'They're coming!' 'Watch out!' The sort of stuff that will make the guards let you get close to find out what's happening."

"Before they shoot me, you mean?" the redhead said wryly.

"They'll think you are one of them. At least, I *hope* they'll think you are one of them. I'd do it, but with a man they'd probably just shoot and send for the clean-up men."

Tom pressed the wrapped Aracta into her arms. "Protect it as if it were a baby. Look back in horror. Look scared."

"I *am* scared."

"Then act it and get Aracta as close as you can. Then fall down—and *stay* down—letting Aracta roll toward those men!"

Tom looked at the alien probe, who peered out through a fold in the plastic with a single lens. "And you do whatever it is you are going to do!"

"Quite, old boy. Fear not, Aracta's here. A good one for the Queen, what?"

"Are you certain it was *literature* he was reading?" muttered Ben. "Sounds like music hall comedy sketches to me."

"Just be thankful he didn't take a fancy to Chaucer or we'd *never* understand him," Anita said. She took a deep breath, hugged Aracta to her, and ran out into the corridor.

She struck the far wall with her shoulder and staggered down the center. "Help!" she exclaimed. "Help me! Save me! They're coming! They attacked Mister Luna and—" She groaned and sagged against the wall, then came off it with a lurch.

The guards had their weapons pointed at her, but they stared in confusion and concern. Anita moaned and fell. Holding the end of the plastic sheet, she rolled the alien ovoid right at the feet of the startled guards.

They stiffened at once. Their weapons clattered to the metal floor as they screamed, clasping their hands to their heads. Within seconds they fell to their knees or collapsed backward, then sank to the ground and were still!

# Chapter Fourteen

Tom and Ben stared at the alien probe's feat, but Aristotle was already rolling past them toward the guard station.

Anita got up and was joined by her two friends. "What did he hit them with?" she asked, impressed.

"Maybe sonics? Some kind of electronic telepathy?" Tom suggested. "We have to be very careful. That creature has capabilities that are unknown to us."

"Do you think he'll turn on us?" Ben inquired.



Tom looked back at the crumpled figures. Aristotle was dragging two of them out of the entrance to the airlock. "Perhaps," the young inventor replied, and bit his lip for a second. "Do you realize that if we get away we'll be locked up in a ship with a dangerously insane personality that is fully armed and unpredictable?"

Anita and Ben nodded glumly and ran to the airlock.

While Ben helped Anita get the spacesuits for them, Tom picked up Aracta and gave him to Aristotle. The robot replugged the probe's wires into his exterior couplings while the others suited up. Aristotle took a laser rifle from one of the guards as an extra precaution. Ben and Tom followed suit.

In a few minutes they were in the airlock. The lock's air froze into a wisp of snow as the bitter cold of space invaded it. Tom had Aristotle jam the mechanism so that no one could follow them out, then they set off into the rough rocks and gullies surrounding the Ceres dome complex.

It took them an hour to get within sight of the *Mime,* sitting on its three sturdy legs, far out on the concrete landing plain.

"Guards," Ben suddenly warned, touching his helmet to Tom's. They did not dare use their radios for fear of betraying their whereabouts. Tom pointed and Anita nodded. She had seen the ten armed men spread out around their ship.

Ben pointed at Aristotle and indicated that the robot could go in and overcome them. Then he grinned sheepishly. Of course, Aristotle had no gas left, and even if he had, it wouldn't work against men in spacesuits. They had no desire to shoot the men with their laser rifles and Aristotle could not break his programing restrictions against harming humans.

Tom put his helmet next to Anita's and motioned for Ben to join them. "If Mohammed can't go to the mountain, then the mountain must come to Mohammed."

Anita frowned. "You have that all turned around."

Tom shook his head. He slid down the side of the small crater they were about to cross and walked over to Aristotle, who had already moved ahead. As Ben and Anita followed, they saw him put his head against Aristotle for several minutes.

The squat robot turned and climbed the crater's side, leaving Tom cradling Aracta in his arms. Soon the mechanoid disappeared behind some rocks.

Ben put his helmet against Anita's. "Do you think when Aracta and Aristotle are hooked up they are talking?"

"At robot speed," she answered. "And we have no idea about what, either!"

They repeated their thoughts to Tom, who just nodded.

"I don't want to seem paranoid," Ben said, "but do you think his insanity could be contagious?"

Tom looked thoughtful, then shook his head. "No . . . but I wouldn't bet against it, either. In many ways, Aristotle has more in common with Aracta than with us." He wrinkled his brow. "But we programed Aristotle and his memory was created by human beings, contributing knowledge and statistics and information."

"Which was organized by you," Ben said. "You selected the basic format of his mind. You were his early training instructor."

"Yes, but from then on Aristotle taught himself. He devoured material!"

"Human material and experience," Anita reminded them. "Aracta is alien. He can't really affect Aristotle."

"New ideas," suggested Tom. "New information. Aracta is a whole new world of information and attitudes. We couldn't hope to keep certain basic premises and human attitudes out of Aristotle's program. Neither could the Skree withhold theirs from Aracta." Tom looked at Anita. "We must always remember that even if something is alien, radically different in appearance and thought, if it is self-aware and intelligent, then it is an entity we must honor. Intelligent life can't be too common out there in the stars."

"Or on Earth, either," muttered Ben.

"Aristotle couldn't be changed by Aracta," Tom said almost to himself. "He could be *expanded,* added to, supplemented . . . but not changed."

"Tom," Ben asked, "what did you send Aristotle to—"

A ship took off far down the field. The flare of its engine made hard-edged shadows, doubling those made by the Sun. The craft rose into the black, star-studded sky on a lance of light piercingly bright.

And exploded!

# Chapter Fifteen

The explosion was silent. The ship, in majestic slow motion, was blown apart, the pieces sent in every direction. Many of them continued out on the course set by the rocket, but some fell back to Ceres attracted by the slight gravity of the asteroid.

"Watch 'em!" Tom said, pointing at the surprised guards.

The men around the *Mime* had thrown themselves down or had huddled behind the landing legs of the white and gold Jupiter Nine. When the last fiery shard had disappeared they got slowly to their feet.

"What did you do?" Anita demanded of Tom.

"I had Aristotle find a ship that he could program to take off and self-destruct. They'll think it was us. Or I'm hoping they will."

"The guards aren't moving," Anita noted.

"Not yet. They're waiting for orders," Tom said.

Five minutes passed, then ten. Aristotle appeared and slipped into the crater. He took back Aracta and plugged him in. Tom spent a few moments with his head against the robot's body, then came back smiling to Ben and Anita.

"He added a nice touch. He faked me giving orders for takeoff—in my voice!—while I accidently left the exterior radio on. And you replied, Ben."

"Aristotle can do imitations?" asked Anita in an awed voice.

"He's heard us all enough and has recordings he can manipulate," Tom said happily.

"I dunno," Ben mumbled. "Maybe machines are getting *too* smart!"

Tom chuckled, his laugh momentarily lost as his helmet broke contact with theirs. "That old fear? Technophobia? Yes, machines can be harmful—if you don't respect them or know how to use them. I haven't forgotten that Aristotle is basically a machine. Oh, sure, maybe the highest order yet achieved—by humans—but he is still a machine."

"I don't know, Tom," Anita said dubiously. "He has a real personality, an incredible amount of knowledge, and . . ." Her voice trailed off.

"But wisdom?" Tom asked. "Heart? Intuition? Intelligence, yes, and maybe some day the line between machine intelligence and man will be blurred and you won't be able to tell . . . or care. But not right now."

"But he's like your son," Anita said.

"No, he isn't," Tom insisted. "I don't want to spoil your illusions, but as much of an achievement as Aristotle is, he is still an invention." He turned toward the guards and pointed. "Look!" The men were leaving!

"When they're out of sight—we go!" Tom gestured to Aristotle, who lumbered up the rocky side of the crater and stood with his head just above the edge. "Anita, you go first. Then Ben. I'll follow with Aristotle. That way we won't get in each other's way as we go to our stations."

They silently watched the guards troop off in response to an unheard radio command. It seemed to take forever for the men to get across the pitted slag field and into the airlock. Tom glanced at the digital watch built into the left forearm of the bulky suit he was wearing.

He had to give them time until they had the inner airlock hatch closed and were partially unsuited. That would prevent them from getting outside in a hurry. Finally, Tom turned to Aristotle and signaled. The robot stepped up higher on the inner crust of the crater carrying a laser rifle he had taken from the knocked-out guards.

Tom slapped the others on their backs and they took off awkwardly in the light gravity and bulky suits. They leaped, rather than ran, and it seemed to take a long time to float back down to the surface. Tom felt very vulnerable and exposed on the flat plain.

Out of the corner of his eye he saw the ruler-straight thin line of red flashing in microsecond pulses from the laser weapon Aristotle had aimed at the nearest of three radar antennae. The mast exploded in a burst of sparks and fell slowly over.

A second thin line of ruby-red lanced through space, stabbing at the sensitive heart of the next radar antenna. It smoked and stopped turning.

Anita had reached the leg of the ship and was climbing up the rungs hand over hand. Ben was right behind her. Tom paused to look back.

Aristotle was still standing on the rim of the crater, aiming the laser and clutching Aracta. "Come on!" Tom yelled, forgetting the robot could not hear him. The red beam sliced out again and there was a spurt of sparks from the farthest antenna. Only then did Aristotle start running. Relieved, Tom grabbed the highest rung he could reach and pulled himself up.

He ripped off his helmet as he went through the *Mime*'s main cabin, thrust his six-foot body into the contoured pilot's couch, and immediately began the countdown. "Computer on!" he said.

"*Ready,*" the computer replied.

"Prepare for emergency takeoff!"

"*Yes, sir.*"

"Tom!" shouted Ben. "There are men coming out of the lock! They have lasers!"

"No course computed!" snapped Tom. "Lift ship!"

"*Yes, sir*!" The *Mime*'s inboard computer was a sophisticated one, though not capable of independent action as was Aristotle. But on the long trip out Tom thought it might be a very good idea if the vessel had the capability of making an almost instant takeoff.

Working for hours, he had reprogramed the

computer to more closely monitor its own internal workings and to keep everything in a state of emergency. All he had to do was give it the command, and, with lightning speed and electronic accuracy, the computer did everything it had to do.

The massive fusion engine was brought from slumber to roaring life.

The ship's radar had been constantly scanning the heavens watching for any objects that might constitute a danger. It withheld ignition for two hundred nanoseconds until a chunk of rock the size of the Cheops pyramid cleared the path ahead.

Then the ship lifted, thrusting against the weak gravity of Ceres.

Tom saw the guards abandon their weapons to leap for cover as he was rammed back into his couch by the acceleration.

The legs folded up and snuggled against the hull of the ship.

Ceres dropped away, rapidly becoming a great smoky-colored, rough-edged ball behind them.

They had escaped!

Tom quickly plotted a course that would take them back to Earth, then he sat back, tired and suddenly sleepy.

"Tom." The voice was Aristotle's and Tom turned to look at the squat metal figure. Across Aristotle's chest was a slash of partially melted metal—a line of near-destruction that went down across his body and across the sleek, indestructible surface of Aracta.

And into one of the lenses.

Aracta was dead!

# Chapter Sixteen

Tom stared at the lifeless egg that had been the emissary from another race.

Dead.

Ben blinked at the ruined probe and Anita was stunned. "Are you all right, Aristotle?" she asked.

"Surface damage only, Anita. It was the first guard out of the airlock. It is all my fault. I turned to activate the hatch mechanism. I should have protected Aracta with my body."

"Aristotle, it was a freak shot," Ben said huskily.



"I had no idea humans were capable of such

accuracy. They have heartbeats, muscular tremors, involuntary reactions, cardio-vascular irregularities, faulty eyesight, and—"

"Aristotle!" Tom said. "It was a freak shot. Nobody's that accurate at that distance! It was an accident! They were probably shooting at the landing legs to cripple us. It was not your fault."

"Tom, as I understand human kindness, you are a kind individual, but there is no escaping my responsibility. I was entrusted with Aracta and I failed that trust. I am truly a flawed mechanism. You should scrap me, Tom. I was a mistake from the beginning. Demote me. I'll run the kitchen for you. I feel capable of turning on and off the garbage disposal."

"Aristotle," Tom said with great patience. "You are not at fault. We would all have done the same. The hatch had to be closed—you can't take off, otherwise."

"I should have anticipated such a possibility."

"Stop blaming yourself," Ben said. "Aracta's had it and there goes the stardrive."

Aristotle was silent a moment, then slowly faced Ben. "Oh, no, Benjamin, not at all. Not if Tom can put the fragments together."

The robot turned back to Tom and indicated the thin wires that still connected him with the dead probe. "We had been having a dialogue on Channels B and C for quite some time. I know exactly where the Skree race lives and why they have difficulties and quite a lot about their history, sociology, planetary botany, zoology, and some of their other sciences."

"Aristotle!" exclaimed Anita.

"The stardrive?" Tom asked, his voice tense.

"That, I'm afraid, was the last transmission Aracta gave me. The beam had melted his main circuit. He started to transmit the specifications, but the overload effect was simply too much for him. He said good-bye and left."

Tom stood up and stared at Aristotle. "Can we construct the stardrive from the informatiom you have received?"

"I could not, Tom. There are too many gaps. But the human mind has vast intuitive powers. From startlingly small data it can draw astounding conclusions. I stand in awe of the powers of human thought."

Tom chewed at his lip a moment. "We have to try, of course."

"Of course. I would like very much to learn from those who created Aracta."

Ben spoke up hesitantly. "Listen, Aristotle, you know we think Aracta was, well, insane?"

"Yes, and there is considerable truth in that. He was aware of it himself. His original crash on Io did some irreparable damage to his vital-functions circuitry. He said it was like watching himself in a play—knowing what he was doing but unable to stop or change certain lines of thinking. There were portions of his being that were quite clear and that could look upon the damaged part but were unable to do anything about it." Aristotle paused, then continued.

"Are you thinking, Benjamin, that the information Aracta entrusted to me is false or somehow warped or misleading?"

"Yeah, something like that."

"There is that possibility, of course, but—"

"Uh-oh," Anita said in a voice that made them all turn to her. She indicated the ship's radar.

A blip was coming after them—a fast ship!

# Chapter Seventeen

Tom swung the *Mime* back toward the asteroid belt. They were going counterclockwise—the direction all the planets went around the Sun.

And the other spaceship was following them.

The belt was not, as many had believed for years, a densely packed belt of miscellaneous rocks. There was actually a great deal of space between the asteroids.

However, the space was not empty. There were dust, pebbles, and small chunks of broken planets which had not yet been pulled into gravitational union with any large rock or asteroid. Had the *Mime* been going clockwise, or against the orbiting mass, these small objects would have penetrated the ship like a high-speed bullet. Dust might have been unable to pierce the metal hull, but the larger rocks would certainly have smashed into the ship. Even going the right way, they could all hear the ringing bongs and thuds on the outer hull as they caught up to or side-swiped some floating debris.

"What's that?" Anita said suddenly from the copilot's seat. "Computer, identify the asteroid straight ahead."

"Yes, ma'am. Configuration of selected subject conforms to that of Vesta. It has a diameter of 503 kilometers, a rotational period of 3.63 years, an albedo percentage of 26.4, and is considered one of the main belt group. It is believed to be basaltic in origin, though no actual sampling has been done. It has a rotational period of 10.7 hours and—"

"Hold," Anita said, and the computer ceased reporting. Left alone, it would have gone through every known fact, then begun on recorded speculation.

Anita looked at Tom. "Basaltic—and the only one, if I remember correctly. The others are siliceous or carbonaceous."

"Then Vesta was probably once the inner part

of a planet," Ben suggested. "The cooled magma from the interior."

"Maybe," Tom said. "But how can we use that to get away?" They all thought a moment as the nearly three-hundred-mile-wide asteroid drew closer.

Suddenly Tom sat up, his face alight with an idea. "Slingshot!" he exclaimed.

"Use the gravity of Vesta to whip us around toward Earth!" Ben said quickly. "Right!"

"Will we gain on whoever is following us?" Anita asked.

"Depends on how powerful their ship is," Tom replied. "We could—"

A thin, red beam shot past the ship, flaring its way through the dust. Tom threw the *Mime* into a turn, then moved it back almost at once. It dodged and dipped, rose and fell in an unpredictable way.

Two more ruby beams of destruction cut through space, narrowly missing them.

The next one didn't miss.

The radar screen went blank. "They've hit the topside dish!" Ben exclaimed, staring out of the forward port. Now they had only the limited and deceptive use of their eyes!

It wasn't that the humans aboard, as well as

Aristotle, didn't have excellent vision and that space was not clear. It was a matter of reference. Since they didn't know how big anything was, they couldn't judge how *close* it was. Without something to refer to that they knew, it was impossible for them to tell the size of an object.

Radar could send a pulse which bounced off the object and returned. The radar could then tell how long it took the pulse to get there and back and—knowing the speed of light—compute how far away something was. Knowing the distance, Tom and his friends could make an educated guess at the size. But without radar they were, in a sense, blind.

Vesta was 300 miles across and how far away? Once again Tom was guessing and he longed for the security that instruments gave him.

Another scarlet line etched itself across the blackness of space, striking a small asteroid the size of a bathtub and heating it so much in a fraction of a second that it exploded.

Tom's frantic maneuvers to escape the deadly rays left him little time to estimate distances and calculate what he had to do.

Vesta came up fast, one side unusually bright, with the sun reflecting off its smooth, black surface. Tom moved very close to give the *Mime* the utmost slingshot effect by adding the gravity pull of Vesta to the ship's speed.

They skimmed so low that Ben almost choked and Anita gave a strangled yelp. Suddenly Tom thrust the control on the directional jets forward and the whole universe seemed to tilt and turn as they whipped around the black rock.

Then they were running sunward with most of the asteroid belt behind them, their main thrusters firing, heading toward Earth.

Without radar they could not determine if the Luna Corporation ship had made the turn with them. But if the pursuers hadn't been ready for the maneuver, they would have overshot, and it was a long way to the next sizable asteroid that they might use as a slingshot.

The *Mime* was ahead and would remain ahead.

Aristotle turned from a side port where he had been observing. "Tom, I registered a flare that may have been a correctional maneuver by the ship from Ceres. They are still in the asteroid belt."

Anita let out a cry of victory and hugged Ben, who was nearest, then leaned over to hug Tom. "You did it!" she exclaimed.

When the excitement had died down and Aristotle had confirmed two more attitude jet correction firings still in the belt area, they breathed a final sigh of relief.

Tom plotted a course into the ship's computer that would take them within Earth's orbit. Only then did he relax and stretch.

As he got up, Aristotle drew close. "Tom, I must ask a favor."

Tom raised his eyebrows. Aristotle had never before said anything like that. He stated wants, needs, or offered courses of action for Tom to select for him, but never a favor.

"Of course, Aristotle, if I possibly can."

With his free hand the robot indicated the lifeless form of Aracta cradled in his arm. "May we give Aracta a funeral?"

Tom blinked. Machines didn't have funerals. They had disassemblies or maybe scrappings. They were cannibalized for spare parts, or sold for the metal or electronic scraps. They didn't have funerals.

"You cannot learn any more from him," the robot said. "I have the plan for the main circuitry in my memory bank. I know the composition of his plastimetal shell. I know 67.4 percent of his memory storage. It would serve little purpose to have an autopsy."

"An autopsy?" Tom gulped. It had crossed his

mind to attempt to take Aracta apart, trace his alien circuits, and try to gain as much knowledge as possible from the first known alien artifact.

But he hesitated. "You know all that?"

"Yes, Tom."

Tom nodded, somewhat embarrassed. If Aristotle said he knew something, then he did. "And you think there would be no purpose in, ah . . ."

"None, Tom. I would like to give Aracta the dignity of a proper burial."

"People might be interested in seeing Aracta."

"I have 1,072 holographic images stored, beginning from before we extracted him from his transportation medium."

Tom still hesitated. It didn't seem right hiding away something as unique and valuable as Aracta, the electronic entity-ambassador from the first known alien race.

"What kind of funeral did you have in mind?"

"I can construct a radio-controlled jet from one of the spare oxygen tanks. I would like to put Aracta in an orbit that will bring him into contact with the primary."

*Cremation,* thought Tom. Right into the Sun. Suddenly his mind was made up. "Of course, Aristotle, go ahead. Would you like me to say something?"

"That would be appropriate to both human and Skree traditions and rituals, Tom. It need not be long. He would have liked a simple funeral, I think."

"Okay," Tom said, slapping Aristotle's arm. "Just call me when you're ready."

"Thank you, Tom." Aristotle did not move for a few seconds, as if thinking of saying more. Then he turned toward the rear of the ship.

Tom looked after him. Maybe Aristotle was more than just a machine? Or was he just aping human conduct? He had read many hours of tape on human anthropology as well as mythology, sociology, and religion. Was his desire to give the alien probe a proper funeral an imitation of human reaction or one of giving a final finish to an unpleasant event?

Tom had little experience with death, and, like most people, didn't like to think about it, but it was an inevitable result of life. But weren't machines different? he thought. People speak of machines dying when they ceased to function, but that is just a personification of inanimate objects. Aristotle was animate and so had been Aracta. Aristotle was already smarter, better informed, and—yes—wiser than many human beings Tom knew.

But he was still a machine!

Electronic life, or the simulation of life, was getting fuzzy around the edges, Tom thought. He had known people so devoid of the joys of life that they seemed like robots and he knew at least one robot with all the delight and imagination of a person.

Tom walked into the captain's cabin. It seemed only appropriate that he wear something formal for the occasion.

# Chapter Eighteen

Soon they were assembled by the airlock. The mood was somber. "Aracta brought us a great prize," said Tom. "He brought us the certain knowledge that we are not alone in the universe, that there is intelligent life out there in the stars. This is one of the greatest messages mankind could possibly receive."

Aristotle carried Aracta in his arms, a small tank strapped to his egg-like shape and a control box on top of that. Ben and Anita stood opposite.

"Aracta came to save the race that created him—a messenger from the stars. He brought hope and knowledge and we pledge to complete his mission to the best of our abilities."

Tom looked at the other two humans and saw they were filled with emotion. Aracta had been a dangerous creature, erratic and paranoid, but his had been a great and noble odyssey.

"We consign him to space, the space from whence he came," Tom said in conclusion. He nodded to Aristotle, who turned toward the air-lock. Ben thumbed the control and the thick hatch slid back with a hiss. Aristotle walked into the lock and stood, immobile, while the inner hatch slide closed and locked.

Tom stepped to the thick glassite port and looked into the lock. He saw the outer hatch open and the air evacuate in a sudden rush of thin snow. Aristotle stood motionless for a moment, then raised his arms and Aracta floated up and out. Carried along by the momentum of the ship, the probe floated not far away until Aristotle activated the air tank. In small spurts of oxygen the tank took the alien farther out. Then Aristotle gave it a final burst and Aracta moved off in a long, lazy spiral.

It would take years before the tiny ovoid of bright metal would be caught by the gravity of the Sun, and still more years before it was pulled down, engulfed, and melted by the extreme surface heat of the star.

Eventually it would be returned to atoms. Alien atoms in an alien Sun.

Aristotle closed the outer hatch and came inside, turning to Tom. "Are you ready to begin? We do not have much time."

They went into the ship's workshop. The *Mime* sped home toward Earth while the young people worked with Aristotle, trying to piece together the mystery of Aracta.

After a particularly tiring session, Tom dropped wearily into a well-padded chair in the main cabin. Anita, who had been in the control cabin monitoring their passage to Earth, leaned forward. "*Well?*"

Ben sauntered in and also collapsed into a chair, leaned back, and closed his eyes. "Boy," he said, "that was tough."

"Come on, you guys. I've hardly seen you for days! What's happening?"

"I'm sorry to stick you with all this monitoring," Tom apologized, "but Aristotle was right. There isn't much time. The enemies of the Skree are coming closer and closer to wiping them out."

"How do you know that?" the girl inquired

while brushing back a stray stand of hair.

"Aracta dumped a mass of raw information into Aristotle in those last minutes," Ben said. "I had a rough time getting it all sorted out. It was like an earthquake in a library followed by a flood. It was all there, but tangled up, misfiled, and mixed up." He yawned and put his hand over his mouth. "How far are we from home?"

"Two days, more or less. You guys have been really out of it!"

"What do you think the great Mister David Luna is going to try next, now that we got away?" Ben asked.

"What can he do?" Anita said. "Or what can *we* do is a better question. It'll be our word against his and he might set it up that we destroyed one of his ships."

"We did," Ben said, and opened his eyes momentarily. "But I don't think he'll complain about that. I think he'll lie low and try his usual sneaky tricks."

"Never mind Luna," Anita said with annoyance as Ben yawned again. "Stop stalling, you bums! What's been going on?"

Tom yawned, too, stretching wearily. "Aristotle gave us all he had, but it was so spotty!"

"The Skree made a lot of assumptions," Ben

said. "For example, they didn't tell us—or it wasn't in the material Aracta gave us—what they look like. They're carbon-based life, just as we are, need a Sun like ours or roughly like ours, but that's all. We know a little about their enemies, but not what they look like."

"It's as if they assume we know—that everybody knows," Tom said. He yawned again, then grinned apologetically. "Sorry, but we haven't had much sleep."

"All right, you guys," Anita cried impatiently, "did you solve the problem of the stardrive or not? Stop beating around the bush!"

"First let me explain hyperspace," Tom said with a grin and Ben moaned. "Ben's mind was bent a bit by this and so was mine."

He looked up at the overhead and arranged his thoughts. "There's space and there's void. Void is where space hasn't gotten to yet. Expanding universe and all that. Outside of the void—sort of on a different plane—is a universe vibrating to a different frequency: hyperspace. It's here all around us—everywhere, but we are not aware of it."

"You don't have the stardrive," Anita interrupted.

"Now, wait." Tom held up a hand. "We felt

that naturally there *had* to be a hyperspace, or subspace, or null-space, or whatever you want to call it. After all, Aracta came here, right? So, knowing it had been done, we proceeded to find out how."

"Then you have it!"

Tom put up his hand again. "Bear with us. Knowing something's been done—even if only once—is an entirely different thing than duplicating it."

"Hyperspace is a kind of shortcut," Ben explained with closed eyes. "You go into hyperspace here and it is the shortest distance to anywhere else."

"Then you do have it!" Anita cried.

"Please, who's telling this?" Tom smiled. "We had only jigsaw pieces and certainly not all of the pieces. A scrap of math, a whole wiring diagram that we still can't figure out, some nearly untranslatable comments, a fully developed criticism of why a hyperspace drive couldn't work! And more bits and scraps of math of this kind or another."

"A mess," Ben muttered. "We had to relearn almost as much as we learned."

Anita looked angry. "Okay, okay, so it was

tough. Now get to the good part. Do you or don't you?"

Tom grinned at her. "We've got it!"

# Chapter Nineteen

Anita let out a yell and happily jumped up. Ben cringed in his seat. "No hugging, no hugging! I'm feeling very fragile right now. Lack of sleep makes my muscles ache."

"You've got the stardrive!" the redhead beamed.

"Tom did it," Ben said. "There was so little to go on. I think only Tom could have done it."

Tom looked embarrassed, but grinned in weary triumph. "Not without you, buddy. You're the one that indexed all that mess. The main thing was that we knew it existed. We knew we weren't chasing rainbows. The stardrive existed and that's what kept us going."

"Are you kidding?" Ben said, opening his eyes. "At least three times I was ready to give up and turn everything over to one of the big labs or NASA or whoever to let them sort it out." He looked at Anita proudly. "Not Tom. He wouldn't give up. He practically made up the entire physics for it all by himself. I'd say it was 90 percent Tom Swift and 10 percent Skree technology."

"Well, I had to adapt their principles to human technology," Tom said softly.

"How does it work?" the redhead asked.

"It sort of dilates real space and you go into this hyperspace," Tom replied.

" 'Dilates'? 'Sort of'? What kind of technical terms are those?"

Tom shrugged and smiled faintly. "We're pretty certain the math and physics are right. We'll have to build a prototype and test it and by then maybe I'll understand why it does what it does."

"Takes surprisingly little power," Ben put in. "It creates a magnetic field—a kind of electronic crowbar—and it forces a portal open in real space."

"A hole in space," Anita said and rolled her eyes in bewilderment. "You guys are going to have to pilot this tub a bit and let me catch up."

"Uh-huh," Ben said, waving his hand aimlessly and yawning again with jaw-stretching energy.

There was silence as they all looked out of the main cabin port at the sprinkling of stars that was the Milky Way Galaxy. Anita's smile faded and after a moment she said, "But what's out there?"

"Millions, *billions* of stars," Ben said.

"And the Skree live on one of them," Anita said softly. "I wonder if they are like us?" She shook her head. "Probably not. The chances of them being human-looking are pretty slim. An unusual chain of mutants, no, a unique chain of mutations led to us."

"The development of any life form is unique," Ben said. "You'll notice that there is a tremendous variety on Earth alone."

Anita laughed. "Oh, dear me, yes. I've seen cacti and bugs and things that I thought didn't develop on *our* planet!"

"But they did," Tom said. "Nature is amazingly diverse. And what would a life form be like that had other kinds of environmental pressures—like the Skree?"

He sat up and called to the robot in the control

room. "Hey, Aristotle! Can you come in and join us for a while?"

In a few moments the mechanoid appeared in the hatchway. "Yes, Tom?"

"Are we on autopilot?"

"Yes. There is nothing within the effective range of our sensors. It is very boring, as a matter of fact. I was just contemplating the fictitious career of Mister Mycroft Holmes."

"Sherlock Holmes' smarter brother," Ben said with a grin.

"Exactly. I was recasting the Holmesian myths with Mycroft instead of Sherlock. For example, in *The Hound of the Baskervilles*, I assumed the position that Mycroft—"

"Aristotle," Tom said. "Sorry, but some other time."

The shiny robot took no offense. "Yes, Tom?"

"Tell Anita what you got from Aracta about the Skree." He quickly added, "I mean in conversational—not mathematical—terms."

"Yes, of course. Aracta had an amazing memory bank. It was a terrible tragedy that it was affected by that radiation. Such valuable and unique knowledge lost." The robot paused a moment, then went on.

"We have no information as to the Skree's

physical configuration, size, or biology. What they gave Aracta was, in effect, a child's version of their history—simplified and undoubtedly presented in a most attractive manner."

Ben laughed. "That sounds familiar, doesn't it? Remember in school how they made most of our historical figures seem so dull because they whitewashed them and removed all their human frailties and color?"

"Go on, " Tom urged Aristotle. He had heard it all before, but each time he had Aristotle recite the information, he gained a little more insight.

"The Skree originated on the planet they call Skranipor. Their sun is Skra. There are seven planets in their system, but only one is habitable without support technology.

"They developed a primitive planetary drive quite some time ago. It was unstated, but I would assume by peripheral data, that this was over 2,000 of our years ago."

"You realize we are talking about the system we call Alpha Centauri?" Tom asked, and Anita nodded.

"It appears here as one star," Aristotle went on, "but it is actually two stars, which is why it seems so bright. It is 4.3 light years away. These stars orbit each other once every 80 years. Their star—which they call Skra—is just slightly larger than our Sun and very similar. The second star is smaller and cooler. There is a third star, Proxima Centauri, which is a red dwarf. Our two systems are approaching each other at 25 kilometers, or about 15.5 miles an hour. In approximately 28,000 years it will be only 3.1 light years away."

"That much we knew without Aracta," Anita said. "What about the people?" She paused and looked puzzled. "Is that the right word? People? Natives? Inhabitants? The creators of Aracta . . . what about the Skree?"

"There are seven planets in the main system, eight in the system of the cooler star, which they call Chiba. It was unstated how many the red dwarf might have. With another system so close, it was relatively easy to reach, once they had developed space flight."

"But not the stardrive?" Anita asked.

"No, that was a recent invention. Perhaps less than a thousand years. They colonized several planets in both systems, though only their home planet was truly hospitable."

"Something like Mars?" Anita asked. "You can live there only if you utilize massive support technology."

"A proper analogy, Anita. The Skree expanded in a direction away from us toward stars which were closer to them. It was there, on a world called Tharcon, that the Skree met a race called the Chutans. By the standards of the Skree—and I would suspect by ours as well—they are savage barbarians."

"The Chutans are an aggressive and ruthless race. The technology they had stolen enabled them to enslave all the life forms in their neighborhood. They nurtured a particular hatred for the Skree."

"Probably because the technology that had enabled them to be so aggressive, and so successful, was stolen from the Skree," Ben said.

"That was my analysis, also," the robot said. "They coveted the worlds inhabited by the Skree. Needless to say, if they could not inhabit a world, it would be all but pointless to fight a war to control it."

"Well, there may be millions of planets out there," Tom said, "but they may not necessarily be within reach."

"True," the robot commented. "Meanwhile, the Skree invented the stardrive and explored and colonized worlds far beyond the reach of the planetary drive stolen by the Chutans."

"Don't tell me," Anita said. "The Chutans stole the stardrive."

"My information is fragmentary, Anita, but I believe a Skree ship malfunctioned in null-space and was thrown back into real space where it was discovered and captured by the Chutans."

"So the savages have a stardrive," Anita said with a shiver. "A crazy man with a laser pistol in the middle of a crowded room!"

"Another good analogy," the robot said. "I am discovering that human speech can be encapsulated into metaphors and analogies for easier and quicker understanding. I am learning from you, Anita Thorwald. Thank you."

"You're welcome." Anita grinned.

"Tell us more about the Skree," Tom urged.

"Oh, yes. It is quite frustrating not having much more than a sketchy history. I have fragments which I cannot connect: words, concepts, and statistics. Who or what are the Chimmies, the High Regent, Princess Eln N'Yn? I have no way of filing these names and facts except in the miscellaneous Skree file. Very frustrating."

Tom sighed and looked at Anita. "Well, if we can make the stardrive a reality, we can find out." Suddenly he grinned. "It's so exciting, I can hardly wait."

Anita Thorwald looked at Benjamin Franklin Walking Eagle and said, "You know, hanging around with you guys hasn't been too dull!"

Ben yawned. "And the fun is just starting!"

Little did any of them realize what would be in store for them in *Tom Swift: The War in Outer Space.*

Tom looked at both of them with a twinkle in his eyes. "You're absolutely right, Ben," he declared. "It's just beginning!"

**THE TOM SWIFT® SERIES**
**by Victor Appleton**

The City in the Stars (#1)
Terror on the Moons of Jupiter (#2)
The Alien Probe (#3)
The War in Outer Space (#4)

**You will also enjoy**
**THE HARDY BOYS® MYSTERY STORIES**
**by Franklin W. Dixon**

Night of the Werewolf (#59)
Mystery of the Samurai Sword (#60)
The Pentagon Spy (#61)
The Apeman's Secret (#62)
The Mummy Case (#63)
Mystery of Smugglers Cove (#64)
The Stone Idol (#65)
The Vanishing Thieves (#66)